Zombies for Everyone

Kimberly Wylie

CYPRESS CANYON PUBLISHING

COPYRIGHT

Cypress Canyon Publishing

Zombies for Everyone

Copyright © 2021 by Cypress Canyon Publishing

All rights reserved.

This book or any portion thereof may not be reproduced or used in any manner whatsoever without the express written permission of the publisher except for the use of brief quotations in a book review.

Printed in the United States of America

First Printing, 2021

ISBN 978-1-7346082-6-7

Cypress Canyon Publishing
222 7th St. West
Brookings, SD 57006
CypressCanyonBooks.com

Table of Contents

Dedication

To Grant who supports me in all things. To Zack who always makes me laugh. And to Brittany who believes I can do anything.

Chapter 1

The moonlight is dappled as it shines through the dense forest surrounding me. Each tree is tall and thin and oddly uniform. The canopy doesn't start for at least a dozen feet above me, a dark umbrella of leaves blocking out most of the full moon I instinctively know would light this place up like daylight, if it weren't for the trees. Ahead of me, though, is just trunks. Not in neat rows. No. That would be too easy.

Where the trunks are incredibly uniform, their placement is not. Some are so close together I can barely squeeze between them. Others are spaced just far enough apart. Many are too close for me to even try to squeeze through. I feel like I'm being guided by their placement— herded. But I have to keep moving ahead.

I have to.

I have no choice.

She has to be here.

The forest floor is shrouded by a blanket of fog. It trickily hides the roots and sticks and vines that seem to be always underfoot. Every step I take, I feel my toe catch on something or my foot step on something uneven, all threatening to send me to the ground. I hear the wind caress the treetops, setting the leaves chattering. It's as if they're laughing at me.

Little tendrils of fog curl up toward my waist as I carefully make my way forward. They brush my fingertips at my side. I feel the cold dampness but do nothing about it. I'm too busy looking around. Looking for a path forward.

Looking for her.

She has to be here.

"Jenna…"

It's a whisper soft voice. Or was it the wind? I stop and focus every ounce of my being on listening. My heart is beginning to pound in my chest. I swear I heard it. I did! But now there is nothing but wind and leaves and the occasional creak of one tree trunk rubbing against his brother.

"Mo-om," I try to shout, to call her, to see if she will answer again. But it comes out a hoarse croaking sound that goes no further than my lips. My mouth is so dry my throat refuses to work properly.

I begin moving faster in the direction where I thought I heard the voice. Every few steps, another tree trunk is in my way, and I'm forced to navigate around it trying to get back on my original heading. The wind sends the leaves a laughing at me again, and I curse them.

"Jen…nnaaa…"

Still soft, the voice comes again. I try to call out again in response, but it's no use. I am completely mute now. The realization of that fact terrifies me. I feel the panic beginning to set in. It sets every nerve in my body on high alert, and my pulse quickens. If I can't call to her, it means I just have to move faster. That's all there is for me to do now.

And I begin to run.

I barrel around trees as quickly as I can, stumbling and tripping on the uneven forest floor that lays unseen beneath my feet. If I go fast enough, I know I can get to her. My ankles will hate me later, but I couldn't care less. I would gladly cut my ankles off completely, if it meant I could get to my mom.

"Jeeeeeeeeeeennnnnnnaaaaaaa."

The voice is only just above a whisper still, but it's now a plaintiff wail. My heart rate increases exponentially in time with my desperation at the sound. I feel it pounding painfully in my chest. But I have to keep going. I have to be quicker.

She is here.

I just have to get to her.

Up ahead, I see a lightening in the darkness of the forest. It must be a clearing. And, between the trees, I think I see a figure. But the fog is getting denser and the figure is hazy. Is it her? Is it even a person?

It has to be her. It just has to be.

I can't see features on the figure, but it seems to be turning its head in different directions as if it were looking from side-to-side. Is she looking for me too?

I *need* to get to her!

Throwing all caution to the wind, I set off at a sprint toward the figure. I bash into tree trunk after tree trunk, ricocheting from one to another like some masochistic pinball, as tree trunks seem to mysteriously pop up in front of me. I feel like I've been running forever, but I'm barely getting closer.

And then it happens.

My toe catches on a root and my body is flung forward as my toe remains trapped behind.

I land hard on my hands and knees. The fog poofs up around me at my impact.

"Jeeeeeeeeennnnnnnnaaaaaaaaaa."

She needs me.

I need to get up. I need to get to her.

But I can't move. Both of my feet are now entangled in roots. My hands have been ensnared with vines. I pull and yank and tug and struggle, but nothing I do works! I'm trapped!

And the figure is leaving!

I see it getting smaller, as if it's walking away. And pure, unadulterated panic sets in.

How could I be this close to her and not find her? How could she be so near, and I would lose her again? I can't lose her! I can't! No! No! No! No! No!!!!

"MOM!!!!!!!!!"

I woke in a cold sweat, my eyes flew open, and I sat straight up in bed. The sheet and blanket were wrapped around my arms and legs, and I struggled frantically to free myself. Finally, the offending covers balled at the foot of the bed, I sat there for a moment and tried to get my bearings. My heart was pounding, and I was breathing like I had just run a marathon. The sick, slick taste of adrenaline coated the back of my throat making me slightly nauseous. Tears ran freely down my cheeks.

A dream.

It was a dream.

I repeated it to myself again and again and tried to get control of the panic. But I knew there was truly only one thing I wanted to do.

I looked over at the clock. 4:16 AM. Good. He'd be awake.

My hands shook as I reached over to the nightstand and grabbed my phone. I hit speed dial for the only contact that was on my home screen.

"Hey, Jen," Kieron's voice was like a warm hug. "Bad

dream?”

"Yeah," my voice croaked with sleep.

"Same one?"

"Yeah…no… sort of," I sighed.

"Do you want to tell me about it?"

Now that I was coming out of the dream fully, I felt stupid. It was just a nightmare, for God's sake. What was I five? No! I was almost 18 years old. I needed to stop being such a baby. I needed to just go back to sleep. I still had almost an hour before my alarm was set. This was ridiculous. *I* was being ridiculous bothering Kieron about this… again.

"Nah, sorry to bother you. I'll see you in a couple of hours."

"Don't be stupid, Jenna," Kieron chided. "Now, do you want to tell me about it, or do you want me to tell you about my game."

Kieron got up at 4 AM every morning to play video games, before he got ready for school. It started with him sneaking in game time, before his parents got up for work when he was in junior high. But then he made some online friends in Japan, and they played every night, so the pre-dawn gaming trend continued long after his folks gave up on trying to monitor his gaming usage. They usually played one of two games—either a multi-player adventure game with elves and trolls and swords and kingdoms to battle for or soccer.

"What are you playing?"

"FIFA."

Oh good Lord.

There were few things more boring than watching someone play a fake game of online soccer (which I can tell you from firsthand experience), but to hear someone *talk* about playing a fake game of online soccer? Yeah, no thanks.

"It was kind of the same as normal," I started. This was not my first nightmare call to Kieron. When I first lost my mom, they used to happen almost every night. Now, six months later, I had been going a few weeks in between. They were always the same. I'm in a forest, and it's like a maze. I can hear my mom, but I can't find her.

So frustrating.

"This time, though, there was someone in the forest too. I could see her. Not clearly or anything, just a figure. But…" and, damnit, my traitorous voice broke. I swallowed and started again, "But I couldn't get to her. Like normal."

I heard Kieron take a breath. "I can't imagine how frustrating this is for you, Jen. I wish there was something I could do, so you'd never have these nightmares again."

I let out a rueful chuckle, "Yeah, so I'd stop interrupting your gaming time, right?" I was trying to make light of it, but I was pretty sure it came out bitter.

"No," he said seriously. "Because I don't like knowing you're upset."

Oh. Gheez. What do you say to that? Oh, I know! You react emotionally and sniffle as the tears began again, because he was being so darned nice.

Check!

"Listen, Jen," he started, "you know it wasn't your fault. You did everything you could."

"Yeah, but I should have found her."

I didn't mean to say it out loud. I really didn't. But it was the truth.

My mom had gone missing six months ago. They had found her Jeep in Bald Hill State Park, but she was nowhere to be found. I had joined the search team for her. We found a trail from the car leading into the forest. Footprints were found under broken pine needles. The trail led about a mile in, weaving through trees, and led to a grassy clearing. The trail continued, evidenced by the bruised grasses where she had stepped.

But then it just ended.

The search team searched for four days.

I continued searching an extra twelve days, until an April blizzard forced me to leave, and I was faced with the reality my mom was dead.

"Pick you up at six?" I said quickly changing the subject.

"Definitely," Kieron replied and let my remark slip into the ether.

There were 150 people sitting in uncomfortable convention center chairs, neatly arranged into rows, separated into two sides by a center aisle. Each chair was evenly spaced directly between the two in front of it. I wondered briefly if whomever set up the room had some sort of jig to get them so even, or if it was just OCD that made them turn out so perfect. The beautiful, clean order of the room was a stark contrast to the chaos I saw playing on many of the attendees' faces.

Their world has forever been changed, I thought to myself.

Most of the attendees were white males. I frowned at this. I don't know why it surprised me. I guess I had delusions of glass ceilings being broken.

Guess I was wrong.

This was a group of large organizational executives and key public figures in the state. There were representatives from huge corporations like Boeing and Caterpillar and Mondelez International. There were representatives from school districts and hospitals and churches. There were even politicians in attendance. I wondered briefly what the exact vetting process was for inviting these specific people out of millions.

I'm sure many in the audience were also wondering too why they had been chosen.

And some probably were wishing they hadn't been.

Others were probably thinking this was all a joke and waited for someone to jump out and tell them they were on some elaborate, prank TV show.

The woman presenting currently, Marlene something or other (I didn't catch her last name when we were briefly introduced) was wrapping up. She was tall and broad-shouldered and commanded the audience in front of her. Although some likely were still doubting the veracity of what they were hearing, Marlene was hard to dismiss. She was in an ivory pant suit and heels much taller than the low ones I was wearing. As she crossed the stage with an elegant, powerful, purposeful walk, it was clear she wore heels quite often.

I did not.

I would be wobbling around like a newborn foal if I had tried to walk in those shoes.

She had a slight East Coast accent—New York or New Jersey I was betting. Her chestnut hair was shoulder-length and held back at the base of her skull with a pearl-encrusted clip. Her makeup was tastefully applied. She could pass for being in her mid-thirties, but she had the air of a woman who had seen and done a lot, so I was guessing she was older. It was clear why they had chosen her to open. She was an eloquent speaker and very comfortable on stage.

I was not.

I hated public speaking.

Loathed it. Would rather poke myself in the eye with a sharp stick and step on a Lego—hated it.

My heart started to beat faster. I closed my eyes and tried to take deep calming breaths. In... and ... out. In... and... out. In... and...out.

"Let's talk about how to apply this information to your organization. Please help me welcome our next presenter, Jenna Sutton," Marlene's voice cut into my zen.

Crap.

People began to politely clap. I took a gulping breath and plastered a smile on my face, which I'm sure made me look like I needed a special white coat with very long sleeves that tied in the back, and crossed the stage to Marlene. She shook my hand and gave me a reassuring smile in return. Great, she could sense my nervousness too.

I turned and looked out at the crowd of expectant faces, as the applause died down. There, in the back of the room, leaning against the wall, was Kieron. He had a big, goofy smile on his face, and he gave me two thumbs up. Somehow his support calmed me, and I turned on the first PowerPoint slide of my presentation.

Chapter 2

"You know, Jen, you're kind of like Buffy," Kieron said as we turned the corner toward the train station.

"Buffy?" I asked incredulously. "Like the vampire slayer?!?"

"Yup," he replied with a smirk.

I rolled my eyes at him. "I am nothing like Buffy."

First, Joss Whedon is genius. If I ever met the man, I'd tell him that, along with demanding he write new Firefly episodes. But, yeah, I wish I were half as cool as his iconic vampire slayer character.

I am not cool—not in the least.

Second, I am the antithesis of a cheerleader. I am not peppy. I loathe the way the cheerleaders, at least at our school, stalk the halls like a pack of hyped up Barbie dolls. Everything is overly funny and overly amazing and overly... overly everything with them. Everything is hyper-exaggerated and fake. Oh so fake. And, so extra.

I gave a mental sigh.

OK, I kind of envied them a little too.

Don't tell anyone.

Cheerleaders always looked 'put together,' as my mom would've put it. My fashion sense centers heavily on jeans and t-shirts. More often than not, my hair is pulled into a simple, functional pony tail.

I also, unlike Buffy, sucked at gymnastics. Seriously sucked. You should have seen me do a cartwheel as a kid. It was not pretty. Now, this didn't mean I wasn't athletic. I had kick ass hand-eye coordination, which made me awesome at some sports—like floor hockey.

That's how Kieron and I became friends, in fact. Seventh grade gym—floor hockey. He was playing goalie for the opposing team. I was left wing. I took a shot and hit him right in the… well, the area where most guys don't want to be hit.

He dropped to his knees in pain. His shockingly blue eyes watered instantly. I felt horrible and rushed up to him to see if he was OK. It was a bonding moment. He's been my best friend ever since. Nothing like a shot to the balls to bond a guy and girl. I honestly don't know what I would've done without him these last few months, and today was just one more day to prove how much I needed him in my life.

Of course, he's occasionally wanted us to be more than friends since that moment too.

Yeah, I don't know exactly what that says about him that a testicle injury caused him to have a crush on me.

But, our timing was always off. I had a boyfriend or he had a girlfriend—mostly he had a girlfriend. Now, almost exactly five years later, we were securely in the Friend Zone. I think it would be too awkward now if things were to change. Plus, I wouldn't want to risk losing my best friend. I've already lost too much. Especially my mom.

I miss my mom.

Even though she was gone a lot for work, the time we spent together was truly quality. She didn't formally start training me until I was 12, but my education began much, much earlier. This meant we spent countless weekends out in the woods—just the two of us. We'd spend days disconnected—no cell phones, no television, no computers, no video games.

It forced us to communicate.

When I was young, because we spent so much time in the woods and stuff, I thought my mom was an outdoorsy person. Come to find out, she was more like me—roughing it to me is a hotel without a concierge. However, the outdoors was where we needed to be, so I could learn things—like how to navigate without a compass, how to track wild animals and even how to hunt.

We never ate what we killed, but it also never went to waste. We'd always stop by Wanda's cabin, and old friend of my mom's, and drop off our bounty. I never saw Wanda. Mom would go up to her door on her own. Apparently she was an elderly woman, kind of a hermit and definitely eccentric. The game we brought her ensured she had food on the table. I always felt good about that—helping someone else. Little did I know my mom was teaching me life skills, not only about the tracking and hunting but how important it was to help others.

This deer season, I'd need to go out to Wanda's on my own. I'd need to tell her about mom. I wasn't looking forward to it. But I hoped she'd answer her door.

But, back to the original topic—yeah, I'm no cheerleader. And, I'm definitely no Buffy. The only things I have in common with the super-cool, fictional Buffy is we're both blonde, we're both in high school... and occasionally I kill vampires along with other things that go bump in the night. It's all part of the job.

Chapter 3

People rushed by us, on their way to who knows where, as we continued to make our way down the busy Chicago sidewalks. I loved Chicago! I really did! Someone once told me, *"It's like New York City—only cleaner."* I hoped someday to go to the Big Apple, to see for myself.

I just wished it were warmer out. Although Chicago in the fall has the advantage of dampening some of the more pungent smells experienced during Chicago in the sweltering summer, it was actually chilly out, especially as we passed under the shadows of the monolithic buildings looming ever-skyward.

Kieron, his dark brown hair flying crazily in a gust of wind, noticed me shiver and asked the obvious, "Are you cold?"

Such a guy thing to ask.

Instead of the smart-ass remark that sat on the tip of my tongue—*No, I'm shivering because I'm really hot. I'm hoping the movement will fan me somehow.*—I replied, "Yeah. I wish I had brought a different jacket."

Of course, today's wardrobe choices were more about style than function or warmth—something rare for me. I usually dress for comfort. Sometimes I dress for what won't show blood or stain as easily. However, trying to 'look professional usually wasn't one of my fashion factors. Today, however, I needed to look the part. And, my dressy wardrobe was pretty inadequate.

"Well," Kieron said giving me a sideways glance, "you look pretty nice today. Very grown up, like when Buffy takes the job as a counselor at the high—"

"For the love of God!" I stopped him mid-sentence. "Would you please stop it with the Buffy references?!?"

I was seriously regretting telling him to binge the series on Netflix last weekend. I thought we could talk about the show, maybe even debate whether Buffy should've ended up with Spike or Angel. I could never have guessed I'd be tormented with a never-ending comparison.

"OK, ok!" he replied, hands up in mock surrender. "I won't say anything else about your similarities to Buffy. Gheez."

"Thank you," I said with a sigh as we continued to walk, glad to finally have that over with.

"How about Anita Blake?" he asked waggling his eyebrows. "Do you like your men with long hair?"

He dodged just out of my reach and laughed, as I took a punch at his shoulder. He's lucky I wasn't seriously trying to make contact. He's a sprinter on the track team, which makes him fast. However, he's not as fast as I am. I could've tagged him if I really had been trying.

As I pivoted from my failed punch, I noticed a black Mercedes S-Class roll along silently behind us, in my peripheral vision. It snuck up alongside of our curb, like a stalking black panther. How long had that car been following us? The hairs on the back of my neck stood up in warning as I stopped walking, turned and stared down the invisible driver behind the darkly tinted glass.

The car moved forward a bit more then stopped. The rear passenger window rolled down and a familiar voice lilted out of it. "Jenna, would you and your friend like a ride?"

Just then, a cold breeze whipped down the street, causing me to shiver even more than before. Yes, a ride in a nice warm car rather than walking the twelve more blocks we needed to go sounded wonderful. However, I knew that voice all too well, and I didn't trust it. It belonged to an old hunter family friend—Cassandra. Even my mom didn't trust her one hundred percent, in the end.

Cassandra—just Cassandra, kind of like Madonna or Sia—was, at one point, not just my mom's best friend but someone she thought of as a sister. I remember when I was little, I used to call her Aunt Cassie. She still liked to be called that still.

Hunters are typically lone creatures. We may choose a non-hunter best friend—carefully, very carefully. Sometimes these relationships are formed with supernatural beings—supes for short. More often though, they're with normal humans, non-supernatural beings—known as nons in my world. Hunters fell between both of these worlds, but with no real supernatural powers it was often easier for us to relate to nons. However, we don't usually form relationships with other hunters. I'm not sure why. Maybe it's because all hunters are jack asses.

No. Seriously. It's true. We are.

Every other hunter I'd ever met was a jack ass. Maybe it was our natural Alpha attitude that made it hard for us to get along with others like us. Maybe it was the fact most hunters are male, and are basically gender equality Neanderthals. They think women should be pregnant and barefoot, and preferably cooking them a nice hot meal or making them a sandwich. Anytime I met one with my mom, they would interact with us with barely disguised disdain.

Then entered Cassandra.

My mom, Allison, was orphaned at the age of ten. If my mom hadn't stayed late at school to finish a diorama of a wagon train, she would've been in the car that killed my grandparents too. Obviously, I wouldn't be here, so I've always been a fan of dioramas. With no other family members, my mom had been placed in child protective services and temporary foster care, until a man came in and offered to adopt her.

Cassandra's father.

Cassandra's dad was a hunter and had been directed by the Consortium to take my mom in. The Consortium pretty much dictates our existence. They're charged with regulating the supernatural world. They ensure peace between the different types of supes. They regulate how supe businesses can interact with nons. They, most importantly for me, also help protect nons from supes and keep the knowledge of their existence secret. As a hunter, we work for the Consortium—although we may take on direct cases, our actions always must be reported and are under the guidance of the Consortium. If we aren't working under the auspices of the Consortium, we aren't allowed to work. Period. For this reason, they really do get to pretty much tell us what to do. So, when Cassandra's dad was told to adopt my mom, he really had no choice.

Cassandra's father resented that.

Although Cassandra and my mom became as close as real sisters, Cassandra's dad was reluctant to train Mom. If it hadn't been for Cassandra refusing to train unless mom was included, my mom would've never become a hunter. I know my mom was grateful for that, and so was I.

About eight years ago, Cassandra was sent to the Caribbean to work as a hunter there. When the Consortium says "Go" you go. Of course, if you were going to be sent someplace, the Caribbean wouldn't be a bad place to go. Sunshine, beaches, warm ocean waves, hunting loup-garous and cocoyas—yup, not bad at all.

When she came back to the States a couple of years later, the Aunt Cassie I had known as a child was gone. While away, Cassandra had become close to a group that still practiced Obeah. She had learned she had had the innate gift of magic, courtesy of some long-forgotten relative. Her mild interest in fortune telling and charm making developed into full-blown witchcraft. Today, she was third in line to be high priestess of the North American coven.

Witchcraft is a big no-no for hunters.

BIG.

Although we often use magical items—charms, potions, amulets, etc. in our work, these are simply tools of the trade. There are too many blurry lines, when a hunter becomes personally involved in supernatural societies. Our job, first and foremost, is the protection of humankind. There can be no questionable loyalties. Although it's known it's extremely rare for a hunter to even try to learn magic, I personally always thought the taboo was such a deterrent we would never know for sure how rare it really was.

When Cassandra returned to the States, the whole supe world was in an uproar. Witches and warlocks from all over welcomed her with open arms. They knew the opportunity a witch hunter in the Consortium would give them. There were protests, but the Consortium put their proverbial foot down. They forced Cassandra to choose—be a witch or be a hunter.

Needless to say, Cassandra gave up her status as a hunter.

Although the Consortium lost one of their best, the worst part was her and my mom were never the same. My mom felt betrayed. I'm sure Cassandra did too. They eventually made up, but something was always off. The Aunt Cassie I knew before was arrogant and cocky and super-controlling. She had her opinions on everything. And if you asked her, she was always right—I told you hunters are assholes. But we had fun together at times. She was often funny and weird and playful. She was eccentric and cool, and I kind of admired her.

When she came back a witch, all the fun side was gone. She was serious and hyper-focused on climbing up the coven hierarchy. Where she was arrogant before, witch Cassandra was narcissistic and a bit frightening. She radiated power. It wasn't malevolent, but it certainly wasn't Glinda the Good Witch either.

"Jenna?" Cassandra's voice came slithering out of her open window again.

I turned and tried to look surprised, like I hadn't heard her before. "Aunt Cassie!"

I stopped, and the car worth more than my house stopped along side me. Busy downtown traffic slipped by on the other side. I walked toward the car as she opened the door and glided over to the far side making room for us to enter. She patted the seat next to her.

"Hop in you two," she said with a smile showing all of her teeth.

All I could think of was—shark!

But, it would be rude of me to refuse, and it was getting colder by the minute. I could now see the driver. He had ebony-toned skin almost as dark as the suit he was wearing. His features were regal, his lips thick and luscious and his eyes like molten chocolate. When he looked at me, all I could think was, "*Wow!*" He was stunning, absolutely stunning. He closed his eyes slowly at me and gave a slight head nod. Somehow I knew he meant it was safe. I turned to Kieron, gave a small shrug and then hopped in to the sedan. I slid to the middle. Kieron slid in next to me and shut the door. The driver caught my eye in the rear view mirror momentarily and my breath caught in my chest.

Immediately—no waiting for downtown traffic to clear when you have magic on your side, I suppose—the driver pulled into traffic and we began moving. I sunk back into the warm, buttery-soft leather seat. This definitely was a lot nicer than walking. My teeth even stopped chattering.

"Where are you two off to? And, why didn't you let me know you were going to be in Chicago today? We could've had lunch," Cassandra said with a pout.

I considered lying to her for a half-second, but knew I would never get it passed her. Whether it be witchy powers or just because she'd known me since I was born, I knew she'd spot a fib. Instead, I went with the truth.

"We're heading to the train station. I spoke at the symposium today," I said simply. Then added, "In place of Mom."

"Oh!" she said, and, for a moment, I think I saw genuine sadness in her eyes. Then it was gone. Her polished, veneer was back, and although she feigned concern, it felt incredibly fake. "It's so tragic she couldn't be here. I'm certain she'd be so proud of you. Stepping into her role. You're a brave girl."

"Thank you," I said because I couldn't think of anything else to say.

"Do you have time for a cup of coffee? I would love to catch up." She placed her red-taloned hand on top of mine possessively. Her hand was cool, despite the warmth of the interior of the Mercedes and the fur (likely real fur) coat she wore.

"I'm sorry," I replied trying to sound like I really was. "I really have to get back home. I have a six-page American History paper due tomorrow. You know—school."

No need to tell her I actually completed that paper three days ago.

"Maybe I can come out to visit you," she offered with

a little pat on my hand. "I feel so remiss not checking on you more often. Your mother would be so disappointed in me." The pout was back.

It actually was kind of an effective pout. I wondered briefly if there was magic behind it, because I felt a little bad about turning her down for coffee now.

"That would be nice," I replied. "I'm pretty busy with school, but text me. I'm sure we can work out a time."

She smiled—more teeth and red lipstick. "Wonderful! Now, introduce me to your young man."

I cringed. My young man? What was this the 19th century? Ugh. "Aunt Cassie, you've met Kieron before, right?"

"Oh!" Cassandra said and her eyes widened in mock surprise. "Is this little Kieron? Hasn't he grown up to be quite a fine looking young man. I didn't recognize you. You two definitely make an adorable couple."

"We're… n-not—" Kieron stuttered.

"Not," I cut in, "dating. We're just friends."

"Yeah, just friends," Kieron confirmed emphatically.

Cassandra frowned at us. "Oh, come on, you two. You can let Aunt Cassie in on your relationship. I can completely feel the chemistry between the two of you. The way young Kieron here has been looking at you, Jenna, is definitely a telltale sign. A young man doesn't watch a young lady like that unless he's smitten."

Smitten? Really?

"And the two of you would have such pretty children. Both of you have lovely bone structure. You're both getting of an age now that when picking a partner you really should consider these things." She paused and then added, "And look at him blush."

"Really, Aunt Cassie," I said absolutely mortified. "We're just friends. Best friends. That's all."

Was she really trying to arrange my marriage based on the genetic potential of how pretty my children would be? This was one step further into Crazy Land than I was used to from her.

I gave a quick glance over at Kieron. He *was* blushing. That blush could mean anything. It could've been because we were just out in the cold. Plus, he always had a little bit of rosy cheeks. It was one of those things that made him kind of adorable. It likely had nothing to do with what Cassandra was saying.

Probably.

"Mmm hmm," she said skeptically as she pursed her lips and looked between the two of us.

Mercifully, the Mercedes glided up to the curb in front of Union Station. Kieron opened the door the moment the doors unlocked and bolted from the vehicle as if it were on fire. He had definitely had enough of Aunt Cassie.

"Thank you for the ride," he called out, already three-quarters of the way toward the station doors.

Chicken.

"Text me about getting together," I said as I too slid out of the awkward warmth and out into the Chicago chill. "And, thank you for the ride, Aunt Cassie. We really do appreciate it."

It never hurts to be polite.

"I'll be seeing you soon," she replied prophetically before the door of her sedan closed with a soft thud. The driver gave me a slow nod, then the Mercedes slipped back into traffic and disappeared amongst the cars.

Kieron waited just inside the glass doors of Union Square. I joined him and we headed down the escalator to the awaiting trains.

"She gives me the creeps," he said with a shudder. "Seriously. Like all the hairs on the back of my neck on end creeps."

"She just takes getting used to."

Of course I knew it was easier said than done. I wondered if I'd ever get used to her myself. Because, Kieron was right. She was creepy. That was a really good word for her. It wasn't something specific though. She hadn't done anything really odd, other than the whole making pretty babies comment. She definitely didn't look creepy. She was, by all standards, very elegant. So what was it? What did make the hairs on the back of your neck stand up?

"I was thinking we should go to Blades and Pints on Saturday," Kieron said pulling me from my thoughts. "They're having a tournament. Free wings to everyone who enters. $250 to the winner. You'll definitely win."

Blades and Pints was, as the name not-so-subtly implied, a local knife and axe throwing bar. I never understood how someone came up with this idea. Yeah, let's let a bunch of people drink alcohol and then throw sharp objects around! But it was very popular, especially on all ages nights. Although drinking age patrons wore wristbands, it wasn't uncommon to see someone I knew from school sipping from a drink.

Kieron was way more overconfident in my likelihood to win though. Although if it were just knives, I'd definitely out throw most people likely to enter. But my axe throwing wasn't quite as consistent. Throwing knives was a necessity in my profession. Being able to attack from a distance was often an advantage. However, it was *way* different from throwing an axe. I was good at axe throwing, not great. And that meant there was no way I was a shoe in for any tournament. Still, it sounded like fun. I could use $250 if I won, and I loved wings.

"What the heck. Let's do it. But don't be disappointed if I don't win."

Kieron gave me a little, playful shove, "I have faith in you, even if you don't."

I didn't have time to respond, because the vibration in my pocket meant my phone was ringing.

The only calls I got were usually from Kieron—and he was walking right next to me, obviously—so, I was fairly certain it was a telemarketer. Probably someone trying to sell me extended warranty coverage on my car again.

The phone number was a local Illinois number though. That was odd. My phone number was a New York number. It was my mom's phone number for years, before we moved to Illinois. Usually telemarketers spoofed a New York number, probably thinking people would be more likely to answer a local unknown call. Little did they know I didn't know anyone in New York, so I never answered a call from there. But, an Illinois number... yeah, I had to answer that.

"Jenna Sutton," I answered simply.

"Ms. Sutton. My name's Keith Pringle. I'm Superintendent of School District 319. I saw your presentation today at the symposium. It was... informative."

"Thank you, Mr. Pringle," was all I could think to say in response to his *informative* comment. It almost sounded like when someone sees a baby who is really ugly and says, '*Oh! What an... interesting looking baby!*" I wasn't so sure 'informative' was actually a compliment. "How can I help you?"

We came off the escalator and headed toward Track 6. The bustling of people around us and the incessant automated "Track 1 – Track 2 – Track 3" coming from each track doorway, over and over, forced me to press my phone closer to my ear and plug the other ear with a finger.

District 319 was my school district. In fact, I thought I'd seen this Pringle guy at our school when we welcomed our new principal. I began to worry maybe this wasn't a hunter thing—but rather a school thing. But he said he saw me at the symposium. Hmm. For a moment, I thought about how weird that was. My school superintendent was in my presentation on 'Protecting Your Organization from Supernatural Activities.'

"We have a… problem… I think you can help us with."

He spoke hesitatingly. I knew that tone of voice. It was the tone someone took when they were worried you were going to think they were crazy—when *they* thought they may be crazy. It's the tone a person took when they were coming to the realization what they knew to be true about the world around them may actually be false, and what they thought was false might actually be true.

I felt a little sorry for him.

I learned about the supernatural world when I was a kid. Heck, I still kind of hoped the Easter Bunny and Santa were real, so hearing there really might be monsters under my bed wasn't too shocking. I can't imagine what it would be like for an adult though.

One day, you're living in a world where things make sense—well as much sense as they can make. You know you're the one that always put the money under your kid's pillow, not some Tooth Fairy. You know vampires are just a stretch of some sadistic guy from history named Vlad the Impaler and are sometimes fictionally glittery. You know the concept of werewolves was likely started because some poor guy had a bad temper and due to hypertrichosis was overly hairy in medieval Europe.

And then you attended a symposium and learned you were completely wrong.

Fairies, vampires, werewolves, witches, warlocks, and all the other boogie men out there were real.

The things that hide under your bed and in your

closet and star in your favorite movies and books really exist and often live right next door.

I wouldn't be surprised if some adults suffered full-on mental breakdowns, once confronted with irrefutable proof of the supernatural world. So, I took pity on the guy and tried to ease his concern that he was losing his sanity.

"Mr. Pringle, don't worry. I know sometimes things can seem a little weird. Why don't you tell me the situation, and I'll be happy to see if it's something I can help with."

Chapter 4

An hour and a half later, Kieron and I pulled up to Phillip General Hospital. It was one of those new hospitals—sleek and modern. The entry area was immense and all glass like an expensive conservatory attached to some mansion, but on steroids. Fancy saltwater fish tanks flanked either side of the entry. These were accented with tropical plants—palms and ferns and giant elephant ear philodendrons—plants that had no business being in Illinois, especially in the fall. Large, comfy leather chairs were placed around the area in clusters. Each grouping with a coffee table for their comfort and use. The ceiling was dozens of feet above making me feel both very small and very insignificant. You could tell this was a hospital whose patients were used to the finer things in life.

I had never even been in a hotel
this fancy.

I noticed the grand piano sitting off to the side. It was a stark a black monolith in a décor dominated by varying shades of grays and taupes. I wondered who played a piano in a hospital? Did they have concerts? Maybe staff and patient sing-alongs? I suddenly had a childish urge to go over and plonk out a few notes on the keys. I mean, you can't leave a piano unattended and not expect someone to give it a go, right?

I giggled at the thought and Kieron frowned at me.

"Sorry," I said not wanting to explain how I amuse myself.

We walked toward the semi-circular desk in the middle of the expansive room. The woman sitting there was dressed professionally, her hair in a tight bun that gave off an air of efficiency. She would've been well-placed at the entry of a high-rise corporate building downtown, not here at a suburban hospital. She eyeballed us as we came nearer.

Thankfully, we didn't have to talk to her. Mr. Pringle gave me the room number of the person we needed to see. We skirted the side of the information desk, walking like we belonged here and knew exactly where we were going. I was thankful I still had my clothes on from the conference, because I felt a little more confident than I would have if I were dressed in my normal jeans and sneakers.

I noticed the clack-clack-clack of my heels on the marble tile floor had sped up a little in my nervousness though. I took a deep breath and purposely slowed my walk.

I do belong here, I reminded myself. *It's a hospital, and I have a very important job to do.*

People in authority always made me nervous lately. I'll admit, I was still waiting for the other shoe to drop with my living situation. I mean, technically I was an orphan, right? When my mom was first pronounced dead, every day I worried I was going to have CPS at my door telling me I had to go live with some random family. But it hadn't happened yet. Maybe it was because I was almost 18. Maybe I had slipped through the cracks of an already over-taxed system. Either way, sometimes people in authority made me worry they'd find out I was a 17-year-old living by myself, and they'd want to do something to change that.

Once we got to the elevator bank, I breathed more freely.

"Are you nervous?" Kieron asked in a hushed tone as he pushed the up arrow next to a set of immaculate, stainless steel doors.

"No… not really," I lied, "… just… it's so fancy in here. Not like a normal hospital. And, that woman was giving me the stink eye."

Kieron laughed. "I can't believe Jenna Sutton is intimidated by a hospital receptionist! After all the things you've faced—THAT uptight, middle-aged woman makes you nervous?"

His laugh intensified.

"OK, haha. So funny; I know." I rolled my eyes at him. The elevator doors opened, and we stepped into the empty space. I pushed the button for floor six then glared at him. "If you're done making fun of me, let's pretend we're professionals for a little while."

Kieron put on a serious face, then smirked as the elevator doors snicked closed, and we began to rise.

We walked passed a nurse's station as we exited on the sixth floor. A round, harried-looking woman in scrubs, behind a high-low curved desk, was rifling roughly through a pile of papers and didn't even look up as we went by. Other medical staff milled about. They also were too involved in their duties to notice two teenagers coming into their world.

It was a long walk down the linoleum clad hallway to get to the room Pringle had indicated. Several of the doors to the rooms were closed, but some were open. TVs murmured quietly from the open doors of some. Sometimes bed-ridden patients could be seen and watched us pass. Other rooms were darkened, blinds closed tightly blocking out the late afternoon sun. Few rooms had visitors, which seemed sad to me. I couldn't imagine anything more lonely than being in a hospital with no one to keep you company. No family.

I mentally steered myself away from that line of thinking. It was not the time to be melancholy.

Room 642 had the door open, and I could see a gentleman standing next to a woman laying in the bed. I knocked softly on the open door, not wanting to startle either of them. The man turned toward me and waved us inside. Kieron closed the door behind us. I loved how he automatically knew this might not be a conversation we wanted medical staff to overhear.

"I'm Mr. Pringle," the man stated reaching out a hand in introduction. "You are Ms. Sutton. I recognize you from the symposium. Although you look younger than you appeared earlier today."

I got that a lot. Most of the time, I chose to simply ignore it.

"Nice to meet you, Mr. Pringle," I replied as I shook his hand firmly, like my mother taught me. "Please call me Jenna. This is my associate, Kieron Nicholls."

Keith Pringle looked like a stereotypical school superintendent. White, middle-aged, average height, not fat, but he had a belly that spoke of more hours behind a desk than out being active. His thin, wire-rimmed glasses sat atop a bulbous nose. His hair was also thin, especially on the top, and a bit disheveled like he had been running his hand through it. He wore a blue suit that was a bit rumpled. In general, he looked like a man who had a lot on his plate and could use a good vacation.

"Thank you for coming so quickly," he began and then paused not knowing how to continue.

I looked to the woman lying on the bed. She was asleep or knocked out; I wasn't sure which. Her breathing was shallow and fast, almost a pant. But, according to the monitor standing sentinel next to her bed, her heartrate was steady and blood pressure appeared to be normal, from what little I knew about vitals. She was hooked up to an IV of something slowly dripping into a line running under the covers, presumably to her left hand.

Pringle just stood there—silent. It had been hard for him to talk to me over the phone; this was almost impossible face-to-face. I could see him having an internal debate. Was this some sort of early senior prank on the school superintendent? I wondered briefly how he had ended up at the symposium earlier today to begin with.

"I'm guessing this is Ms. Pruett you told me about on the phone," I started. "Why don't you tell me what happened."

Mr. Pringle took a deep breath and moved to the far corner of the room, where a built-in bench lined one wall and a chair sat next to a small table. He motioned to us to follow suit. Kieron and I sat on the bench, while Pringle took the chair.

He took a deep breath and began, "Yesterday morning, Ms. Pruett was found outside the school, by one of the students and a staff member. She was on the ground, unconscious and..." he paused and took another deep breath, "two of her fingers were missing."

"Missing?" Kieron asked.

"The doctor said bitten off."

"So," I interjected, "you think the thing that did this was supernatural? Could've been a stray dog or a coyote?"

Coyote attacks weren't common. But with all the new construction going up in what used to be farm lands surrounding the Elmview burb I lived in, it meant they were definitely being seen more and more. On the phone, Pringle had said Pruett taught English at Elmview South. That was right next to a new subdivision and a cornfield. A coyote bite was definitely more probable than something supernaturally nefarious.

"I thought the same thing yesterday morning, when I came to visit Ms. Pruett and talked with the doctors. But then I got a call last night saying she wasn't doing well and had fallen into a coma. I came right away and her injury, well… it looked different. The doctors feared it was an infection.

"Then I sat in your talk today… and you mentioned the signs… and well, I think you should take a look at her. Maybe… maybe I'm wrong." He motioned to Ms. Pruett's prone form, but made no move to get up himself. He just sat their wringing his hands worriedly.

I got up and walked over to Ms. Pruett. I pulled back the covers covering her left hand. It was fine—healthy and whole. Five slightly chubby fingers. Not one of them gnawed on.

"Sorry," Mr. Pringle said quietly, "the other hand."

I walked around the bed and pulled back the sheet covering her right hand. Before I even got to her hand, I could see the greenish-gray marks trailing up Ms. Pruett's forearm. The Lichtenberg figures looked like delicate ferns tattooed into her flesh but were slowly creeping up her arm and would eventually seek out her heart. Her hand was covered in a bandage, but I was sure if I were to remove it not only would I find two missing fingers, but the hand would be almost entirely green-gray, with blackened tissue necrosis starting already nearest to the bite wound.

Definitely a zombie bite.

Crap.

"You were right to call me, Mr. Pringle," I said as I began to rummage through the inner pocket of my suit jacket. I set a small bag of sea salt, a vial of vinegar, and a cloth bag filled with a variety of crushed herbs and things I probably didn't want to know what they were on the edge of the bed.

"Bowl," I said to Kieron, but he was already next to me with a pink, plastic kidney-shaped bowl. I always wondered what those were for in hospitals. Was a patient supposed to throw up in it? Pee in it? Wash their face in it? It didn't seem practical for any of those things. And why the weird shape? Why not a round or oval bowl? These are the types of random things I ponder about when I'm dealing with life and death situations. I was pretty sure it was a coping mechanism.

I opened the cloth bag of weird witchy healing and dumped all of the contents into the bowl, before tucking the cloth bag back into my pocket. The last thing I needed was to accidentally leave it here and have some medical person start to analyze it. Next was the sea salt. And, finally, the vinegar. It immediately didn't smell good. But, in my experience, that was a good sign.

I slipped the plastic bag the sea salt had been in over my fingertip and began to stir the mixture. A soft knock on the door was heard just before it opened.

"OK Ms. Pruett." The overly cheerful voice preceded the round nurse we had seen at the nurse's station when we got off the elevator. "It's time to check your vitals."

Kieron was in front of her in a heartbeat, blocking her entry. "I'm sorry," he fake whispered overly loudly so both Pringle and I could hear him, "but we're right in the middle of a prayer service. Could you please give us 15 minutes?"

"God is our refuge and strength, an ever-present help in trouble," I began loudly to cover the sound of the scraping of salt crystals on plastic as I stirred.

Luckily, I had been blocking the view of my concoction with my body and my head was already down looking at the bowl. I lifted my eyes only to Mr. Pringle, and he proved his intelligence by quickly bowing his head and clasping his hands in prayer.

"Therefore we will not fear, though the earth give way and the mountains fall into the heart of the sea, though its waters roar and foam and the mountains quake with their surging…"

"Oh! I'm so sorry to interrupt," the nurse said quietly. "Ms. Pruett can use all the prayers she can get. I'll be back in a few minutes."

The nurse quickly scurried out of the room, and I finished mixing up the paste-like mixture in the bowl. I set my makeshift finger glove in the side of the bowl and gently turned Ms. Pruett's arm over and exposed her inner forearm.

On this side, the greenish-gray spidering along her skin, were almost to the crook of the poor woman's elbow. This was not a good sign. In fact, it was possible I was too late.

I really didn't want that to be the case.

Too late meant there was no way to stop Ms. Pruett from turning. Her turning meant I'd have to take drastic measures. Drastic measures meant a bolt to the brain. And that would be a whole other set of logistical challenges.

I would need to come back to the hospital, because there was no way I could do that in front of Pringle. He'd freak out for sure. Then I'd have to call in a cleaning crew, which is bad enough when you just have a body to deal with, but they'd need to deal with Pringle, the nurse and medical records, for sure, probably police records too. I'm sure someone reported the bite to the police. Oh, and maybe animal control.

Ugh.

That was a lot of paperwork, and I did have classes and homework and things like laundry to deal with. I did not have time for that much paperwork. I hated Consortium paperwork. So I said a little prayer that what I was about to do would work. It was a selfish prayer, but a prayer that also benefited Ms. Pruett, because, if it worked, it meant she'd live to see tomorrow's sunrise.

I reached up and pulled the hidden knife from the necklace I always wore. It was a gift my mom had given me when I was fourteen and probably the handiest knife I had. Shaped like an arrowhead, no one ever expected with a little tug came out a two-inch, razor-sharp push blade made of pure silver. I had gotten in many places with that blade I shouldn't have. And more than one supe had seen the wrong end of it, when they thought they had had the upper hand.

Today, it sliced through the upper bandages of Ms. Pruett right hand, exposing her wrist to me and a small chunk of her palm. The part of her palm I could see was entirely gray, with a darker purply-gray just peeking through on the edge.

Yup, I might be too late.

I took the knife and ran three quick slashes across her wrist. Blood began to immediately ooze from the fresh wounds. It was a brick-red and too thick.

"What are you doing?!?"

I hadn't seen Pringle watching. I should've warned him. He lunged across the bed to grab at me. I wasn't sure what he thought he'd accomplish by that, but thankfully I didn't have to worry about it. Kieron was paying attention and had already positioned himself at the foot of the bed, making it easy for him to come around and pull the older man back.

"Stop," Kieron said as he wrapped his arms around Mr. Pringle and leveraged him back toward the bench. Pringle likely had 40 pounds on Kieron, but Kieron had youth on his side. "Let her finish, or you're going to kill that lady."

I slipped the plastic bag back on my finger and

scooped up a glob of the salty-herby mixture and rubbed it into the wound. Instantly, the noxious smell intensified and an acrid smoke rose from where the goop met Ms. Pruett's blood. I quickly added more, rubbing intensely. I was thankful the woman was completely out. Salt in a wound is never fun. Having someone scrub it into a wound was enough to make even the strongest person scream in pain.

I knew this from firsthand experience.

Two more scoops and scrubs and the smell was so bad, I was gagging, and Pringle and Kieron were coughing. I glanced up at Kieron, he still had Pringle's arms pinned to his side in an awkward backward bear hug. Pringle had stopped fighting, his face sheet white and eyes wide despite the coughing, but neither I nor Kieron trusted him to remain calm.

The plastic bowl empty, I could see the salve already sinking into the wounds. A few more minutes and there would be no evidence of the stinky stuff left. It would be gone and either Ms. Pruett would be healed, or I would be making a trip back to the hospital tonight to pay her a not-so-nice visit.

I pulled the bandages back together the best I could and turned her arm back over. I pulled the cover back up and indicated to Kieron with a nod to let the superintendent go. He released the man with a, "Behave," muttered warning.

"What… what was that?" Pringle stuttered. "What did you do?"

"That was Ms. Pruett's only hope," I replied simply. I wouldn't have gone into details, even if I was allowed to—which I wasn't.

"Now we wait, right?" Kieron asked.

"Yup," I said, just as Ms. Pruett moaned loudly next to me.

We all turned to her, as she let out another loud, low,

sorrowful moan. It was the sound of someone in absolute agony—a sound that vibrated your bones and pulled on your heart strings. Her head turned one way, than the other, slowly back and forth, with her eyes still closed.

Another moan, and I noticed her heart rate increased from a steady 72 to 95.

More head turning continued, this time faster—side-to-side-to-side-to-side. Pruett's mouth opened, and this time the sound was almost a howl. Her heartrate was 106, and her blood pressure had sky rocketed to 190/100.

Monitor alarms started to go off, alerting hospital staff something was very, very wrong with their patient. It was only a matter of seconds before we'd run out of time being alone. Stupid technology. As if on cue, the round nurse from earlier flew into the room, flinging the door wide.

"Step out of the way!" she ordered as she bustled quickly over to the monitors, hitting buttons to turn off the alarm.

"Mwwha…" Ms. Pruett mumbled, head still turning side-to-side but much less frantically.

"Ms. Pruett," the nurse leaned in to her.

With a huge intake of air, like a person who had been under water too long, Ms. Pruett's eyes flew wide open. The nurse stumbled back in shock.

"Ms. Pruett," she tried to regain her composure as she returned to her bedside, "can you hear me?"

"Wha…what…hap…happened?"   Ms.   Pruett stumbled, squinting up at the nurse.

"You had a bit of an accident," the nurse said in a soothing voice, "but it looks like you're out of the woods now. I'll be right back with the doctor."

The nurse turned and headed quickly for the door and then stopped before exiting. She turned to the rest of us and said, "I don't know what prayers you said, but I think we've all just witnessed a miracle."

As she scurried off down the hall, Kieron quickly closed the door again. I needed some answers from Ms. Pruett before the doctors came back.

"Ms. Pruett, my name's Jenna. I'm a consultant for the school district. Can you tell me what happened Wednesday morning?"

"I... I don't really remember," she said closing her eyes again and turning her head away from me. I'm sure the last thing she wanted to think about was the attack, but this was life or death for others now.

"Ms. Pruett," I said in the most authoritative voice I could muster, "look at me."

She complied.

"It's very important you try to remember. Anything you can tell me may be very helpful." Then, with some thought I added, "We're going to need this information to ensure you get paid for the time off you'll need. If I don't have any information, I can't even begin to process your claim."

"Well," she said slowly, "I drove to the school and arrived at five o'clock, like normal."

Money—that will motivate people every, single time.

"And I parked in my normal parking space, on the west side of the building, by the corn fields. You know, the ones that separate the school from the new subdivision going up?"

"Yes, I'm familiar with that area. Then what happened?"

"I got out of my car, grabbed my purse from the passenger seat. then went up the steps to the C corridor staff door. Then..." she trailed off. Her eyes had closed again, but this time her brow was furrowed in concentration.

"You were on the steps, in front of the door..." I

prompted.

"I was just about to enter the code to unlock it…" she slowly continued, "… and then… something grabbed me. I don't know. My coat? Maybe my lunch bag? I don't know. But, I remember being pulled backward and that feeling…you know…when you're falling? That's…"she paused again. "That's all I remember. Other than waking up in the hospital."

She looked around the room; agitation grew in her voice. "But it wasn't here. It wasn't this room. This isn't the room I was in" She was becoming more desperate for answers as the realization sunk in she had lost a significant amount of time. "Where I am? Did I fall asleep? Did someone move me? Where did the room go where I was?"

"I'm sure that was the emergency room, Ms. Pruett," I said soothingly. "You're safe now. You're at Phillip General. You're in very good care. Thank you for telling me what happened. That's going to help a lot. Mr. Pringle will make sure any time off you need is compensated. And, of course, all medical bills will be covered in full. Right, Mr. Pringle?"

Mr. Pringle stepped closer to the bed, still white as a sheet and visibly shaken by the last ten minutes of his life. "Yes, yes," he assured her, "of course I will."

"Oh, Mr. Pringle!" Pruett startled, "I didn't even see you here. I really need to put my glasses on, but I have no idea where they've gone."

She went to pat at her head, to check if she had left them there, when she pulled up her bandaged right hand. She looked at it in shock, noticing immediately the blood-stained outer bandages near her wrist.

"Oh my!!" she said weakly, and the color washed away from her face. "What…what happened??"

Thankfully, the round nurse returned at that moment, with what appeared to be a doctor.

"We'll go look for your glasses, Ms. Pruett. The doctor's here and will explain everything."

I signaled for Kieron and Pringle to follow me out of the room and excused us as we passed by the doctor. He looked at us quizzically, but had more pressing concerns with a newly awoken patient who was starting to sob uncontrollably.

In the middle of an empty parking lot, where I could be sure to see someone before they could overhear us, I gave Pringle the lowdown as the sun began to dip toward the horizon.

"You were right for calling me," I began. "That was definitely a zombie bite. In fact, if we had arrived much later, she would've turned."

"Into a zombie?" he asked incredulously.

"Yes."

"So… zombies are real. Like Walking Dead zombies," he continued. He shook his head back and forth ever so slightly, still in disbelief.

"Mr. Pringle, listen, my job is to keep this community safe from the things of nightmare and legend—things most people will never know really exist, if I do my job right."

"But you're so young," he interrupted.

A second reference to my age. That always set my teeth on edge, when someone commented about how old I was—or how old I was not. I think it bothered me less when other hunters made chauvinistic comments about my gender. I just chalked those up to them being idiots. But my age? That was like nails on a chalkboard to me. I could ignore it once, but two comments in less than the span of an hour?

Maybe I was a little worried I was still a bit green, a

bit wet behind the ears as it were. I knew I wasn't technically an adult, but I'd done more and seen more in my short 17 years than most people would in a lifetime. Plus, I was very, very well-trained. I knew that. I reminded myself Pringle didn't know me from Adam. It wasn't really out of line for him to worry about a teenager handling something so serious, right?

The little devil on my shoulder whispered, *"Yeah, but he just saw you cure a woman and prevent her from turning into a zombie! Shouldn't that give you some street cred?"*

"I know I'm a bit young, Mr. Pringle," I said stiltedly, the irritation thinly veiled in my voice, "but this is the job I was trained for, as my mother was before me. I was literally born to do this, and I do it quite well, as you just saw. If you'd like to handle this on your own, I'll leave you to it and wish you good luck."

"No! No! I need you! I mean… thank you," he stammered. "I do appreciate what you did for Ms. Pruett. Umm… we never did talk about your fee—"

"Sadly, this job's not over," I interrupted. "There's still a zombie on the loose near one of your schools, and it needs to be stopped before it hurts someone else—or worse."

I didn't want to tell him the 'worse' wasn't just someone getting killed. The 'worse' could be a full-scale zombie outbreak. For all I knew, there were more people who'd already been bitten. There may be someone being bitten right now. If I didn't find the zombie and deal with its victims soon, Elmview would turn into this century's Roanoke.

I'd need to go to Elmview South and see if I could find the trail. That would be the best place to start. Hopefully, they had video surveillance, like my school—Elmview North. Kieron was a whiz at all things techy. I'd need him to review the footage, while I did the old-fashioned hunt for clues.

I went over these details with Pringle and explained I'd likely need to be at the school tomorrow too, to help identify if any students or other teachers had been bitten. I'd also have to call into the Consortium, when I was done here, and let them know to keep an eye on police reports and hospital admittances. They'd also want the details of the contract, so they could ensure they got their cut when I was paid.

I pulled my phone from the back pocket of my slacks and asked Pringle for his e-mail address. I sent my standard contract off to him, with the inclusion that both Kieron and I would receive full credit for any assignments or tests we missed while at South. If I found the zombie quickly and there weren't any new victims, this would be over in a day or two. If others had already been bitten, well the exponential nature of the spread could mean we were in this for the long haul. I just wanted to make sure this job wasn't going to jeopardize either my or Kieron's GPA.

I definitely didn't want to repeat my senior year because of a zombie.

Pringle e-signed the document, and I had it back in my inbox moments later. He said he needed to make some calls to alert the substitute principal, so he could meet us at the school.

"I just don't know what I'm going to tell him," Pringle said to me. I could see the worry on his face. He didn't want to tell anyone else there was a zombie on the loose. He'd think Pringle was nuts. I didn't want him to tell him either, because the fewer people who knew about the supernatural world, the safer we all were.

"Tell him there was an assault on Ms. Pruett, and we're contracted by the school board to investigate. It's the truth without you having to worry about sounding like you're a half-a-cup short of a full box of Fruit Loops. But make sure he gives us carte blanche to anything we need to do our investigation—at any time of the day or night."

"OK, OK. That sounds like a good plan. Stevens is a good guy. He's really helping us out until we can get a new principal for South. Tows the line. If I tell him to give you full access, he will."

"What do you mean 'new principal?'"

"Freak accident. Ms. Cowell, the previous principal, slipped and fell down the stairs. Hit her head on the way down and a few hours later, she was gone. Very tragic. That was last week. So we've been scrambling to fill the position. We have a few people in the running; Ms. Pruett was one of them. We like promoting educators into administrative positions. They have a unique perspective that oftentimes career administrators don't have.

"Anyway, Stevens is the principal for Reagan Elementary, just down from Elmview South, so he's been helping out until we fill the position."

"Good. Make the call. I'm going to go home and change and we'll head right over there afterward. Won't take more than thirty minutes. OK?"

"OK," Pringle said nodding his head in agreement. "I'll call Stevens right now."

"Perfect," I said as I stuck out my hand to leave. "We'll get this taken care of. Don't worry."

Chapter 5

I changed out of my 'grown-up' clothes and was now in my favorite pair of jeans, t-shirt and a light jacket. Kieron and I got out of my little Audi TT. I called her Baby Car. What? Don't tell me you've never named a car. She was silver and almost as old as I was, with miles well into the six digits, but she was still sporty-looking, fun to drive, dent-free, and not a spot of rust on her despite the salt-laden Illinois winter roads.

Most importantly, she was free.

A client gave her to me as payment for my services, when I saved his organic cucumber farm from a family of kappas living in his pond. The makeshift pond was really more of a muck hole. It was where their cows enjoyed standing—and pooping. It took a week to get the smell of manure out of my nose, and I ended up throwing away the clothes I had worn. But Baby Car made the job well worth it.

I loved Baby Car. And I knew, despite her age, she still turned heads when I drove down the street. Adults especially were more than a little impressed. The man standing in the main parking lot of Elmview South was no exception.

"Nice car," he said with a nod of approval as he walked toward us, as we got out of the car.

"Thank you," I said sticking out my hand. "You must

be Richard Stevens. I'm Jenna Harris. This," I indicated with a nod of my head, "is Kieron Brady."

Aliases were important in situations like this, when we had to work with nons and keep them in the dark. The last thing I needed was for Stevens to discover Kieron and I were students at the rival high school. That would open a whole can of question worms I didn't want to answer.

The Jenna Harris and Kieron Brady aliases were chosen for a couple of reason. First, we wanted to keep our first names the same. It was less likely we'd screw up and call each other by our real name that way. There was nothing more awkward than when someone called out your alias first name and you ignored it, because you didn't realize they were speaking to you. We chose our last names based on people we admired. Both Kieron and I agreed it'd be easiest for us to remember. I chose Harris after one of my favorite authors, Charlaine Harris. Kieron chose Brady after who he said was, and I quote… "The best football player ever to grace the field"—Tom Brady. I had no idea who that guy was, but apparently he was still pretty famous even though he didn't play anymore.

"It's nice to meet you, Ms. Harris," Stevens said shaking my hand. He then reached for Kieron's. "You too, Mr. Brady."

He looked incredibly similar to Pringle. Middle-aged, white, short on hair, long on beer belly. The school district could definitely use a district-wide Get Fit Challenge. So far, too many of their staff looked like they were one side of bacon away from a heart attack.

Stevens looked at us quizzically. "Aren't you two a bit young?"

Teeth. On. Edge.

I took a deep breath and looked him levelly in the eye. It had been a long day.

"You aren't inquiring about our age, Mr. Stevens, are you?" I said as I cocked my head to the side and narrowed my eyes at him. "Because I'm not sure that's very appropriate."

Stevens eyes widened as he realized he was likely treading on some pretty thin HR ice, with people contracted by the school board. He back peddled as quickly as he could. "Oh, no! No, no, no, no, no! I meant it as a compliment. I apologize. It came out completely wrong. Let's start over. It's very nice to meet you. Would you like to come inside to the school first? Or where would you like to start? I defer completely to you expertise."

Better.

"Thank you. I think I'd like to start where the attack happened. If you can show me which door Ms. Pruett was at, that would be helpful. Then, if you would please take Kieron to review the security camera footage—I'm assuming they have security cameras here?"

"Oh, of course, they have security cameras," Stevens started. "Some of them have been giving the school a little trouble I believe, but the west side exterior cameras were working fine the other day."

"Great."

"If you want to follow me around the building in your car, it's a bit of a walk."

He wasn't lying. I knew Elmview South was larger than my school, but I had no idea it was this big. At the front of the building, by the main parking lot we had pulled into, was a single-story building with the front entrance of the school. Like my school, this part of the school housed security screening through the entrance, security offices, the nurse, and the administrative offices. Looming behind this building was a behemoth of a three-story building, with eight corridors of classrooms radiating from its massive body. With the small administrative building, then the massively larger main building with eight legs coming out from it, Elmview South looked like a giant spider.

I followed Stevens, in his white Toyota Corolla, passed the head of the spider, around the body then passed two of the legs… I mean corridors jutting out. He pulled up across from the end of the third corridor and got out. Kieron and I followed suit.

"This is Ms. Pruett's car," Stevens said pointing to a late-model, blue Ford Focus he was parked next to. "And this is the door she was going into when she was attacked by the coyote or dog or whatever it was that bit her."

The door was a windowless metal security door, with the letter "C" stenciled on it. It was reached by a short series of concrete steps.

"Can you tell me what happened, Mr. Stevens?" I asked hoping to glean some new information.

Regretfully, it was pretty much the same story I had already heard. Ms. Pruett was unlocking the door to come into the building when 'an animal' attacked her. She was pulled backward off the steps, hit her head and went unconscious. The janitor was the first to find her, and when a student came along, he rushed off to get help while the student called 911.

Nothing new.

"Thanks, Mr. Stevens. I'm going to do some looking around, if you can please show Kieron the security footage now."

They both got into Stevens moderately-priced sedan and drove back to the front of the school. I watched them turn around the second wing of the school and disappear out of sight, before I took a deep breath and started to look around.

Ms. Pruett had backed into her spot. To the passenger's side of her car was a large trash dumpster. Behind her car was a corn field still full of drying corn stalks. The night breeze blew across them, rattling their fibery bones.

Twenty-five feet—that was the entire distance between Ms. Pruett's car and the edge of the steps. Someone must have been very close to her, to come up behind her before she even got the door unlocked.

I crossed the narrow road and walked passed the area where Pruett must have landed. The sidewalk along a small stripe of landscaping had a brownish stain on it. Someone had tried to clean it, but blood can be trickier to remove than most people realize, especially when it comes to a porous surface like concrete. The amoeba-like shape was gruesome in the yellowish, institutional parking lot light above. I climbed up the steps and turned around to face into the parking area.

The wind whipped a stray clump of hair into my eyes. I reached up, pulled my pony tail elastic off my hair and raked my fingers through it. I turned briefly into the wind to get all of the stragglers into place and refastened it before surveying the scene.

The night air smelled like fall—crisp, cool and the lightly sweet scent of decaying leaves... and trash. A slight smell of rotting garbage emanated from the large, metal box next to Ms. Pruett's car, despite the fact the lid was closed There was a half-moon shining in the sky. If I hadn't seen the zombie infection firsthand, I could've ruled out werewolves. That was no help though.

Where could a zombie have been while Pruett walked up to this door? That was a more pertinent question.

Zombies ambulated at different speeds. When newly turned, they actually moved almost live person fast. They could even clumsily run, if they were on the chase. As they aged, they became less coordinated, which slowed them down quite a bit. This kind of made sense, because even though their corpses were magically protected from decaying at normal speeds, they did still decay. This included muscles and ligaments. So, depending on how old the zombie was, he could've been off in the cornfield or he may have needed to be almost right behind Pruett, to attack her in the short time span between the car and school door.

If it was an older zombie, you would think someone would've reported the smell—Ms. Pruett, the janitor, the student. Someone should've noted something. So it must've been a newer zombie.

Unless they just thought it was the trash.

OK. Not helpful.

I looked out again. Really there were only two places a zombie could've come from, no matter what age they were. Behind the trash can or in the cornfield—it had to be one of those two spots. I considered perhaps around the backside of this wing, between it and the fourth leg of the building. But that would've meant the zombie would've come into Pruett's peripheral vision at some point. Although it's possible she wouldn't notice someone coming up to her in the early morning hours, it's not likely.

The wind gusted into me as if it were nudging me. I looked more closely at the cornfield. From this vantage point, four feet off the ground at the top of the stairs, I could just see over the tops of the golden stalks standing sentinel in the partial moonlight. The field itself turned out to be actually quite small, approximately the width of a football field. It was the last struggling vestige of what this area used to be not even five years earlier—Midwestern farmland. This little strip of nostalgia now served as a barrier between the school and a quickly growing neighborhood of tract homes.

But the positioning of the field meant something else. I lightly stepped down the stairs, shaking my head. There went my one hope of an easy solve to this job. Because of the hundreds of cookie cutter homes on the other side of the cornfield, there was a myriad of paths running through the stalks of corn. I had hoped the zombie had escaped through the dying stalks. It would've made it incredibly easy to track him by just looking for a flattened trail. Sadly, the field already looked like intricate corn maze from the kids going back and forth between the school..

I pulled an LED flashlight out of my pocket—no need to run down my phone battery—and flipped it on. I did a sweep around the trash dumpster. Nothing unusual. I then tried the nearest entrances that had been smooshed into the corn. I hoped to find a patch of skin caught on the sharp leaves, some blood or even a dropped off fingernail.

Nothing.

With a sigh, I got into Baby Car and pulled around to the front of the school to see if Kieron had found any leads.

"142 cameras and over a third of them are out? That's ridiculous! This school isn't even five years old!"

I heard the frustration in Kieron's voice as I rounded the corner into the security office. He sat at a bank of security screens, most of them scrolled through a live feed of different positions around the school. The screen directly in front of Kieron, however, was paused.

It wasn't the highest quality image I'd ever seen, especially with the movement of the subject. The lack of sunshine, given the early hour, in the video also wasn't helping the situation. Despite the less than perfect image though, it was clearly a car Kieron had paused on. More importantly, the car was obviously a Porsche 911. Although Elmview South was in a more expensive part of Elmview, I was sure there would only be a limited number of Porsches on campus, especially at 5:08 in the morning, according to the time stamp on the surveillance video.

"I agree," Stevens said, unaware I had come into the room. "I noticed that too when I started helping out last week. I put in a requisition to have the broken cameras fixed. The district says they should still be under warranty. The security company says it's not a warranty issue. We sit in the middle with blind spots all over the school as a result."

"Any luck finding the coyote?" I asked

I admit, I got a little too much satisfaction out of watching both of them jump as I startled them.

Kieron spun around in his chair and rolled his eyes at the smirk on my face, "No sign of the coyote. The camera directly over the door into corridor C was down. I'll need to go through all of the other feeds to see if I can catch it on another camera. But Mr. Stevens was able to identify which student came to Ms. Pruett's aid that morning. He recognized the car."

The Porsche belonged to a one Tiffani-Amber Blair. She was head cheerleader for Elmview South.

Of course she was.

"I also found one video down corridor D from inside the school," Kieron added. "You can definitely see a janitor pushing a trash cart out the door before Ms. Pruett showed up. The second camera catching the back half of the corridor isn't working. But to make matters worse, the camera on the outside of D stopped working right after the janitor went through the door. So we pretty much just have eyes on the first half of the hallway."

I could hear the frustration in his voice. It was ridiculous. How could such a new school be operating with such defective equipment?

"We think it's a wiring issue," Stevens chimed in. "Quite a few have gone out when they were jostled. Guessing when the janitor went out the door, it slammed behind him and knocked that one loose."

"So is that the janitor who helped Ms. Pruett?" I asked.

"We assume so," Kieron replied.

"OK, that's something. Mr. Stevens, I'm going to want to talk to both the janitor and the student in the morning. Can you arrange that tomorrow? Mr. Brady and I will be back tomorrow morning."

"Oh," Stevens sounded a bit put off. "I figured you'd just check out the scene of the accident and that would be it."

"Unfortunately," I said in my most conspiratorial tone, "the district wants us to do a full investigation. Was it a coyote? Was it a neighborhood dog? What can be done to prevent it from happening again? Is anyone going to sue the district? The whole nine yards. Such an ordeal for a simple bite, right? But you know how they are."

"Oh, I absolutely know how they are," Stevens said knowingly. "I can set you up in the principal's office. It's not a problem. And Mr. Brady is more than welcome to comb through the camera footage from either in the security office or I'm sure we can get him access to the archives on the computer of his choice."

"Perfect. We really appreciate your help with this. We'll be out of your hair in no time; I promise," I assured him.

"Hopefully this whole school will be out of my hair soon. I have my own school to run. I don't need this district red tape on top of everything else I have on my plate."

I made sympathetic noises, said our goodbyes and a few minutes later, Kieron and I walked across the parking lot to Baby Car and sat inside. Stevens got into his blah mobile and drove away.

"So no luck?" I turned to ask him before starting the car.

Kieron turned toward me, and it happened.

Sparks.

Not literal, set-stuff-on-fire sparks.

Metaphorical, make your heart race, attraction to someone sparks.

In the half-light of the street light filtering into the car, he just looked so damned handsome. And, for the first time that evening, I could tell he was wearing cologne. That was weird. I hadn't noticed it earlier.

But it smelled amazing!

I wanted to nuzzle my nose into his neck and just breathe him in. Maybe then I could nibble on his neck a bit and feel the heat of his skin against my lips. My heart was beating so fast—flittering in my chest like a rabid hummingbird trying to break out. Worst of all—I felt like giggling. How the heck was it appropriate to giggle right now, when I was on the hunt for a zombie who could be killing someone right now?

But, boy, did I want to giggle now.

Kieron was just looking back at me. I had no idea if all of these lusty thoughts were playing across my face, but before I knew it, his hand was gently caressing my cheek. Without thinking, I leaned into his touch. My eyes slid closed, as I savored the feel of the warmth of his hand against my skin.

What the hell was I doing?!?

"So, yeah, no sign of the zombie?" I said pulling away from Kieron, focusing on the parking lot in front of me, and turning the key in the ignition.

"Uh," he cleared his throat, sounding like he too was trying to regain his composure. "Yeah. No sign. But there are several more cameras to check. I'll look at them tomorrow. You know. Look for something…"

His voice trailed off.

I chanced a half-glance at him as I pulled out of the parking lot. He was pointedly looking out the passenger window.

It was awkward.

Awkward as heck.

"Yeah, I think it came in through the cornfield, on the opposite side of the trash can. You know, from where Pruett parked. The angle—of the door—Pruett would've, or I suppose I should say should've, seen something coming from the other side, in her peripheral vision. And, if it was on the other side of the wing, it would've had to cross right to the side of her—again, peripheral vision. So cornfield."

I was rambling. Why in the world was I rambling like an idiot?

Kieron continued to look out the window and made a non-committal sound. The rest of the ride was in silence. All I could think about the entire ride home was how near Kieron was to me. How easy it would be for me to reach over from the shifter knob to take his hand.

We pulled into my driveway. Neither of us had said a word the entire ride. I hit the garage door remote and pulled into the garage.

"Crud! I totally forgot to take you home!"

Me distracted much? Nah!

I shifted into reverse when Kieron reached over and stopped my hand. My heart began to race again, and I kept my eyes forward fixed on the garage wall.

"It's OK," he said. "It's decent out. I can walk."

He only lived three blocks away, but at that moment the last thing I wanted him to do was go home. Kieron's hand was still on mine, on the shifter. I needed to move my hand to pull the emergency brake and turn off the car, but I didn't want to do anything that might cause him to move his hand. I didn't want to do anything that would break this connection.

"Jen," Kieron continued.

I turned toward him, and it happened.

He kissed me.

His lips were warm and smooth and firm. He tasted like spearmint gum, and I became light-headed with the giddiness of it all. Every fiber of my being screamed "Yes! Yes! Yes!" It felt so right. Him. Me. This moment. Why hadn't we done this earlier? Why had we waited years? My eyes closed, and I melted into the kiss…

… until my feet slipped from the clutch and the brake and the car lurched backward, crumpling the garbage can in the corner of the front of the garage, before the engine abruptly died.

"Oh my God!" I threw the emergency brake and scrambled out of the car.

Kieron was out a moment after me. He pulled the slightly crushed, plastic garbage can away from the car, and we both knelt at the back passenger's side corner to inspect the damage.

"Looks like you got lucky," Kieron noted, running his hand along the back bumper feeling for any damage. He continued feeling for damage along the underside and came to a halt.

The next thing I knew, Kieron was on his back, with his head under the back end of my car. I watched him reach into his pocket and pull out his cellphone. He flipped on the flashlight and shone it on the underside of the car. A moment later he emerged with a bundle of canvas. String was wrapped around it with feathers and bones interspersed in the binding. He held it out to me, tentatively with two fingers like it was something icky.

"Weirdest road kill debris I've ever seen."

I took it from him and inspected it. I had seen something similar a few months ago, at a college down near the Kentucky border.

"That's not road kill. It's a charm bag."

"A charm bag?"

"A lust charm bag, to be specific," I said inspecting it closely.

I walked over to the garbage can, bent and mangled, opened the lid, and pulled my push knife from my necklace. I slid it into the canvas bag, letting the contents spill into the garbage. I then sliced through the twine binding the bones and feathers together and dropped it on top of an empty pizza box from two days ago.

"Who would put a lust bag under your car? And why?" Kieron asked.

Good questions.

"No idea," I said honestly. "They're expensive, first of all. Not many witches or warlocks can even make one. It's definitely not the kind of thing most people would willingly give away."

"The weird just keeps coming with you, Jen," he joked as he playfully punched me in the arm.

He wasn't wrong.

Chapter 6

I hit snooze for the third time. It had been a rough night. The lust bag was bugging me. Who would've put it there? When did they do it? And, more importantly, now that it was destroyed, why did I spend all night thinking about how amazing that kiss had been?

Ugh.

I showered quickly and dried my hair. I pulled my hair back, but instead of my usual plain, black hair tie and high ponytail, I kept it low and fastened it with a fancy hair clip at the base of my skull. There. That looked professional, right? I moved into the bedroom and rifled through my mom's closet for something appropriate to wear. This is where all my grown up clothes came from. The sight of her clothes, running my fingertips along the neatly hung items, brought a lump to my throat.

I missed her.

I missed her every single day.

I didn't think that would ever change.

Tears welled up in my eyes. One broke free from his brethren and rolled down my cheek. I scrubbed it away quickly with the back of my hand. I didn't have time to wallow in self-pity. I had a job to do. If I wanted to honor my mom's memory, I needed to do that job well. I grabbed a sunny yellow pants suit—fake it until you make it, right—and got ready to go to work.

Kieron was downright chipper on the drive in. He was definitely a morning person. I definitely was not.

He hopped into the car with a "Good morning, sunshine!" and handed me a Yeti tumbler. It was filled with hazelnut coffee, extra sweet, just the way I liked it. That helped a little.

He didn't say anything about what happened the night before. Nothing about the lust charm. Nothing about the kiss. As we drove, we talked briefly about the plan for the day. He would continue to search the security camera footage. I would interview the cheerleader and the janitor. Hopefully, we'd find out where the zombie went. It was actually quite telling that there didn't appear to be any other attacks.

There are two basic types of zombies—infected and made. The majority of zombies are the infected kind—kind of like those you see on TV. They're created when a person is bitten by a zombie. Of course, unlike fictional, pop culture zombies, if a victim dies before they become a zombie, they're just dead. New zombies are transformed, like the path Ms. Pruett was on. The victim is bitten and is infected with the virus. The victim does actually die, as the last step in the process. However, if a victim is so severely bitten by a zombie, say they bite a jugular or a femoral artery and the victim bleeds out before the transformation is complete, the victim just plain dies.

It's actually a good thing it happens like this. Well… good, I suppose, is a subjective term here. It's not so good for the victim. Anyway, typically zombies are pretty blood thirsty, which means they normally don't leave victims alive. It's this one simple fact of supernatural nature that has probably saved the world more than a hunter like myself, from a true zombie apocalypse. If the victims they killed rose as zombies, well that would mean they'd multiply exponentially and pretty much make my job impossible.

The second type of zombie is a made zombie. These are far more rare. A healthy, well as healthy as dead people get, dead person is raised from the grave by magic. Voila! Zombie!

This is very serious magic. It's really a form of necromancy. The practice, I hesitate to call it an art, was developed in Haiti, by Mambo Mama Cecile.

She had come in from the fields and happened upon her husband, Renol, and his mistress in a… shall we say… 'compromising situation.' In a fit of anger, she swung her scythe, meaning to kill the other woman. However, her husband jumped in the way to stop her and ended up with a scythe through the belly. Mama Cecile was so distraught about killing her beloved, she spent all of her time trying to develop a way to resurrect him.

After three days, she succeeded. Renol awoke, but as a zombie—and very hungry. Three villagers lost their lives before Mama Cecile found she was able to control him. Eventually, Mama Cecile's instruction to Renol wasn't specific enough, and he turned on Mama Cecile herself. Renol then began the first infected zombie outbreak, including one of his infected offspring biting a sailor who was on a boat heading to America.

Yeah, supernatural history I'm pretty well-versed on, but please don't ask me anything about non-supe history. What dates World War II were, where Custer had his last stand, all of that is pretty non-existent in my brain.

Stevens met us at the door. He handed us two lanyards with passes to hang around our neck. We walked into the front entrance, and security thankfully was not on duty yet. I didn't want to explain half of the things in my bag, or the knife at my ankle and small of my back.

Stevens guided us into the administration area. One gal was already seated at the entrance desk. She had a large stack of papers she was looking through a bit frantically. She stopped what she was doing, sliding a finger as a placeholder between the sheets, and greeted Stevens. Stevens made an introduction, telling her our names and letting her know we were with the school board. He instructed her if there was anything we needed, she should accommodate us.

"Betsy is new, but she's doing a great job," Stevens complimented. "She helps us with a lot of things, including acting as our general secretary and receptionist, ensuring we have substitutes when needed, student attendance, that sort of thing. But she's also really excellent at doing just about anything you could ask. I couldn't have gotten through this last week without her."

I noticed the blush on Betsy's cheeks, as she gave an *Aww shucks!* kind of shrug and replied, "Thanks, Mr. Stevens. I appreciate it."

We went behind the reception desk and walked down a rectangular hallway. Offices branched off the outer side of the rectangle. The center looked to be a large conference room, with a big table and a dozen or so chairs arranged around it. The upper part of walls of this room were glass, so you could see all the way through to the opposite hallway and its corresponding set of office doors.

Stevens stopped in front of one of the doors along the back hall and unlocked the principal's office. He handed me the key.

"I have a pretty busy schedule—going between both

schools, but if there's something Betsy can't help you with, please don't hesitate to call me." He handed me a card with his phone number on it before turning around and heading back toward the reception area. Kieron headed off toward the security office, and I went into the office I had been allocated.

It was a generic school office. Nothing really screamed principal's office. A desk sat toward the back, with two, wooden uncomfortable-looking chairs positioned in front of it and a large, ergonomic-looking office chair behind it. A window dominated the back wall. The blinds were open, and I could see it looked out onto a beautiful maple tree. Its leaves were already on fire with yellows, oranges and reds. Beyond it was the drive that went around the school and then the cornfield. It was a pretty view—kind of bucolic. On the left side wall was a filing cabinet. A computer monitor sat on the corner of the desk, a keyboard in front of it. A multi-line phone sat on the opposite corner.

All pretty standard issue.

I set my laptop bag on the desk and pulled my laptop from it. I plugged it in then started it up. I put my finger on the fingerprint scanner. A message followed, emerging one letter at a time, as if someone was typing it.

```
GREETINGS PROFESSOR FALKEN.
SHALL WE PLAY A GAME?
 - TIC-TAC-TOE
 - BLACK JACK
 - GIN RUMMY
 - HEARTS
 - BRIDGE
 - CHECKERS
 - CHESS
 - POKER
```

- FIGHTER COMBAT
- GUERRILLA ENGAGEMENT
- DESERT WARFARE
- AIR-TO-GROUND ACTIONS
- THEATERWIDE TACTICAL WARFARE
- THEATERWIDE BIOTOXIC AND CHEMICAL WARFARE
- GLOBAL THERMONUCLEAR WAR

The IT people at the Consortium were way too into old movies and, obviously, had way too much time on their hands. I chose GLOBAL THERMONUCLEAR WAR and looked steadily into the webcam. I waited, without blinking.

RETINAL SCAN COMPLETE.

It was a two-step biometric security—a necessary evil to keep supernatural data secure. Hey, it worked. I'd even seen it in action.

I had my laptop on a table in Starbucks a couple of months ago. I had been doing research on Bakrus—yeah, NEVER enter into a deal with a Bakru—and got up to get another coffee. I put my laptop into sleep mode. When I came back, I see a guy bending over my seat, staring wide-eyed and open-mouthed at my screen. I came around him to see what he was gawking at. Images of him—him at work, him with a woman, him putting gas in his car, him with another woman, him putting something in his jacket in an aisle of a convenience store, him standing in line at the post office, and so many more—flitted across the screen in rapid succession.

Then the screen went black and a message appeared...

TAMPERING WITH NSA COMPUTERS OR OTHER DEVICES ARE IN VIOLATION OF FEDERAL STATUTE 18 U.S.C. 1030. AUTHORITIES HAVE BEEN NOTIFIED.

The screen then reverted back to black. The man stood slowly, looked at me and then bolted out the door. I almost wet myself I laughed so hard. I had no idea how they did it, but when you think of the phrase 'IT wizard,' well it's literally true with the Consortium IT staff. And I was thankful they had implemented these security features. Too many jerks out there like that Starbucks guy, or worse.

I opened up my notes for the case and my e-mail. I shot Kieron a quick message, asked him for whatever footage he had from cameras (that worked) at the time of the attack. I was 95 percent certain Kieron would catch something, if there was something to be found on the video footage. But that remaining five percent meant I needed to at least double check for myself. His reply came quickly—

Already on it.

Attached were three videos clips. I opened up the first. It showed the view of one of the entrances of the parking lot. I watched as Ms. Pruett's car turned slowly into the school in the pre-dawn glow of the morning. She drove through the parking lot and then moved out of camera range. I continued to watch an empty parking lot for several minutes. I fast forwarded the video through until I saw Tiffani-Amber's 911 come tooling into view and then quickly out of view, as she zipped across the parking lot as well.

The second clip appeared to be from a camera just around the corner. It also caught Ms. Pruett's car driving in the parking lot, but this angle showed it backing into the parking space Kieron and I had seen it in the night before. I watched her get out of the car, start to move away then turn back toward the car. She reached in across the front seat, her butt the only part of her visible now in the video. I few moments later, she straightened back up and I could briefly see she had her purse and a folder in her right hand. She shut her car door with her butt, pointed her keys at her car with her left hand, presumably to lock it.

Ms. Pruett stopped once again and patted her chest with her left hand. Then she patted the top of her head. There she found her glasses. Instead of putting them on, she tucked them quickly into her purse. She finally crossed the roadway toward the school. She made it just to the edge of the pavement as she exited the video frame.

A few minutes later, the Porsche rolled into view and parked next to Ms. Pruett's car. Tiffani-Amber slid out and threw a tiny backpack on over her shoulders. She was wearing a short, tan leather jacket—that I admit I was a little jealous of—and had a plaid scarf around her neck. She tossed her long, chestnut hair back and checked her reflection in the car window before she turned toward the school. She came into full view as she got to the end of her little 911, and I clearly saw her stop, in the middle of the parking lot drive. This must've been the moment she spotted Ms. Pruett.

Instead of running to Ms. Pruett's aid, as I imagined most people would, Tiffani-Amber just stood there for a full 30 seconds. She looked around—for someone? For something? She said something. Then she slowly made her way forward, almost tip-toeing, and was out of the shot.

The third clip was inside the school. The halls were empty for several seconds and then a janitor could be seen pushing a rolling trash cart into view. He was dressed in a vivid orange jumpsuit. It reminded me of something you'd see prisoners wearing. I wondered briefly if this was a required uniform or a personal fashion choice. The man was clearly paid by the hour. He wasn't in any hurry to get his job done as he sauntered slowly across and then finally out of the frame. The time stamp on the film was 4:54 a.m.

The clip continued for sixteen long minutes with nothing happening. I fast forwarded it. I started to wonder if

I was missing something when a short kid with floppy, dark hair entered the frame. He was wearing a black jacket that was two sizes too big for him and black jeans. He slouched down the hallway, his head turning back and forth, as if he was expecting someone. He too exited the video frame and was gone.

The video clip kept playing, so I knew there was something else Kieron wanted me to see. Sure enough, three minutes later, a person I hadn't expected to see came into the camera's view and walked down the hall. It was one of the most hated teachers of Elmview North—Mr. Durban—also lovingly known as Mr. Douche Bag.

Douche Bag Durban had been an English teacher at Elmview North and an assistant coach for the football team. He was the worst teacher in the world, unless you were on the football team. If you played football, you pretty much were guaranteed an A in his class, even if you simply wrote your name on a piece of paper and turned it in for an essay. Everyone else? Well, he was an asshat. There was no other way to put it. I did a report on Orwell's *1984* and he gave me a C- because I had written 787 words, not 750 words, as he had requested.

He had been vying for the vice principal position at North last spring. Rumors were when they brought someone in from outside the district he threw a literal fit in the teacher's lounge. The stories ranged from him tossing chairs around to throwing himself on the floor and crying. I doubted either were true, but when school started this year, it was a relief to find out he was no longer terrorizing the non-athletic students at North.

I had heard he had transferred to a different school. I didn't know it was *this* school. But here he was, walking down the hall toward the camera, head down and focused on his cell phone. He seemed to be speaking to someone as he walked.

The clip continued and the hallway was empty again until the janitor came back into view. He was moving slightly faster than earlier, but still not with any real sense of urgency. More importantly, he had the dark stain of blood on the front of his bright orange uniform. Although the resolution wasn't the greatest, as the janitor came closer to the camera, I could see the poor guy wasn't feeling good. He looked a bit out of sorts—a little shocked. Of course, I couldn't blame him. You find a co-worker with two fingers bitten off, and most people would feel a bit queasy. He continued out of frame and the clip ended.

I sat back and sighed. I was hoping we'd get a glimpse of the zombie, at the very least. But at least I now had three people I needed to talk to—Tiffani Amber, the janitor and the kid in the black jacket.

Chapter 7

"Betsy?" I said over the phone's intercom, hoping I pushed the right button.

Nothing.

"Betsy?" I said again trying a different button.

Still no answer.

"Betsy?" I tried pushing a third button.

Silence.

OK, this was stupid. I clearly was not smart enough to use an intercom system. I'd have to do this the old fashioned way—walk down the hall. I got up and headed out of the office and turned directly into a large wall of flesh.

"I'm so sorry," I said immediately and looked up... to see Mr. Douche Bag himself. Durban was tall and broad-shouldered. He had the type of build where you knew at one point in his life he probably was really ripped, but years of bad diet and lack of exercise turned all that bulky muscle into just plain old-fashioned bulk. His hair was jet black and slicked back. I always wondered if he was going for a Count Dracula vibe. He was wearing a long-sleeved, blue button down with white French cuffs and a pair of black slacks. Snazzy.

"Who are you?" he asked giving me the hairy eyeball.

"Jenna Harris," I said stretching out my hand. Good. He didn't recognize me from his Junior English class last year.

"My partner and I are here from the school district, investigating the accident with Ms. Pruett the other day."

"Carl Durban, Dean of Students," he said pompously taking my hand and shaking it briefly. His hand was clammy, and his handshake was limp. I hated that when men did that. Instead of shaking your hand like they would another guy, they just place their hand gently in yours, like they're too afraid they're going to hurt you. "Aren't you a little young to be working for the school district?"

Of course he'd be one of those people. But at least—

"And I swear you look really familiar." He squinted his eyes at me, as if he was trying to bring my face into focus.

Danger, Will Robinson! Danger!

"I think I *have* seen you," returning his scrutinizing look. "At a school board meeting or two, now that you mention it. Dean of Students, you obviously attend those," I hedged.

"Hmm… yeah, that's probably it. Are you working in there?" He nodded at the principal's office door I had just come out of.

"Yeah, just until we get this report wrapped up."

"Well, don't get too comfortable. That's going to be my office soon."

Wasn't he the confident one?

"Really? Well, congratulations on the promotion."

"Oh, it's not set in stone yet. But it will be," he replied cryptically. "My current office is this one." He thumbed toward the door next to the one I had come out of. "It's not a far move, but it will be a big one. Now, if you'll excuse me. I have important things to do."

I'm sure you do, Carl. I'm sure you do.

"Betsy?"

"Yes? How can I help you Ms. Harris?" Betsy stopped highlighting a spreadsheet she had in front of her.

"I was wondering if you could come into my office and take a look at something for me, for a moment."

"Sure thing. I'll be there in just a minute."

I headed back to my office. True to her word, a minute later there was a light knock on the office door.

"Come on in," I called out as I forwarded to the spot on the video I wanted to show Betsy.

"What can I do for you, Ms. Harris?"

"Can you take a look at this student and let me know if you recognize him?"

"I can try," Betsy replied as she came toward the desk. "I just started here this school year, so really don't know very many—oh."

She stopped as she looked at the image on my laptop I had turned toward her.

"That's Thomas Evanson," she said simply.

"You know him?" I said surprised. I had forgotten Stevens had said Betsy was new to the school staff.

"Yes, ummm," she started uncomfortably, "he's…well, he's not the best student here at Elmview South. Let's just put it at that. I'm really not sure what I can say. You being with the school district and all.

"I'm new," she continued rambling awkwardly. "I guess I already mentioned that, right? But I just—I just don't want you to think I talk about the students. I'm sure that's probably against the rules, right? But Mr. Stevens did say—"

"Thank you," I smiled at her and cut her off to end. "You did perfectly fine."

I could see the tension in her physically release at my reassuring words.

"I have one more request. I'd like to speak with

Tiffani-Amber Blair and this Thomas Evanson when school starts, please. If you could call them to the office, for me, when the bell rings, that would be really helpful."

"Sure thing! I can definitely do that," Betsy responded eagerly.

"And there was this janitor on staff Wednesday morning," I said as I changed the image to a screenshot of the janitor from the third video clip. "I would really like to speak with him as well."

She looked at the clip carefully and said, "I'm not sure who that is. But we only have two janitors on staff at a time, so I'm sure it won't be hard to figure out who he is."

As Betsy turned to leave, I stopped her. There was one thing still leaving an unpleasant taste in my mouth. "One last question. Carl Durban. I understand he's slotted to be the next principal. Any idea what the hold up on the promotion is?"

"Carl?" Betsy laughed and came a little closer to the desk. "Can I say something? Off the school district record?"

"Of course, Betsy." Oo! I loved gossip!

"Between you and me," she said conspiratorially. "Carl's a bit delusional. There's no way he's going to get that spot. There are too many other really good people that are interested in it—people who have been here for years.

"I suppose when he doesn't get it he'll be packing up. I heard that's why he left his old school, because he got passed up for a promotion. And good riddance to him. He's kind of a pompous ass. Again, off the record."

"I got that from our brief encounter," I smiled and nodded sympathetically. "I couldn't imagine him running a school, so this is good news."

With my thanks once again, Betsy scurried out of the office.

While I waited for Betsy to bring Tiffani-Amber, Thomas or the janitor to my office, my next step was to check the Consortium records to see if there had been any other zombie attacks I somehow had missed. Honestly, I did try to keep up on the supe activity, but the Chicagoland area had one of the highest concentrations of supes in the country, which meant there was quite a bit of activity to keep abreast of.

A quick search of the database showed no confirmed zombie attacks in the last three years. There had been a handful of suspected cases, the most recent looked promising. It was actually a camper who had been killed in Rock Cut State Park in September. The state police had called it a bear attack. That struck me as odd. I didn't think there were bears in Illinois anymore. Could this have been a zombie attack that was misfiled?

I opened up the file on my computer and looked at the details. There was a video attached in the folder. Apparently the camper had been streaming a Facebook Live event at the time of his demise. I clicked the video and watched as a forest opened up in front of me. The victim was standing just about 25 feet from the edge of a small river. It gurgled happily in the background. Sunshine danced off its ripples, as birds and insects provided the soundtrack.

He had sixteen friends watching.

"This is where I caught two nice-sized fish yesterday, guys," the filmer's voice cut into the serene scene as he made his way closer to the river. "Hopefully, I'm lucky again today."

Little heart emojis trickled up from the corner of the screen, as a few of his watchers approved.

As he moved through the brush and the shoreline

became fully visible, he stopped in shock.

"Oh my God!" he whispered excitedly. "Do you guys see this?! It's a little bear! Oh wow!"

Some wow face emojis began to appear, along with more hearts.

There on the water's edge, just up the shore, was a black bear cub. It was splashing in the water, swiping playfully at unseen fish under the surface.

"I'm going to try to get a little closer," the victim said quietly as he started to sneak forward toward the unsuspecting cub.

A few thumbs up likes and a heart appeared, but a few comments began to appear too.

> Dude! Don't be dumb!
> Yeah I'd get outta there.
> Here kitty, kitty!
> Better make sure mom's not around.
> Hey, Boo Boo!

Ignoring his friends, the victim creeped closer and closer. Occasionally, he panned left and right—up and down the river. The cub remained clueless to the man's approach, as he focused on the game of trying to catch dinner.

How close is he going to get? I wondered to myself. *And isn't he worried about momma bear?*

As soon as I thought that thought, a rustling sound blocked out the happy splashing of the baby bear. The victim swung around at the sound. "Shit!" was the last words heard as the screen was blacked out momentarily. The next moment, a swirl of blue, green and brown overtook the frame as the man's phone went spinning out of his hand. The picture resolved looking up into the cloudless blue sky, the only thing marring it was a blade of grass that had bent in front of the lens upon landing.

The victim's friends were in shock.

Are you OK?????
Shit! Shit! Shit!
Dude say something!
Someone call 911!
Anyone know where he is exactly? I'm calling right now.
I think he said Rock Cut. Tre, are you still there?!
Hang in there, man. Help's coming.
Curl into a ball! Play dead!

Gone was the serenity of the soundtrack only a few moments earlier, instead screams of fear and guttural growls were heard off in the distance. The sound of tearing fabric was heard just below the "No! No! Noooo!" of the victim. Then there was the snap of bones and a final piercing shriek and the sound of the river returned—along with the occasional sound of tearing flesh and rumble of something large and off-screen.

I continued to watch, looking at the sky and that single blade of grass, and then I heard something moving closer. Snuffling noises and then a big, black nose came into the screen, steaming up the lens, as momma bear checked out the weird thing on the ground. A big, clawed paw swiped at the camera and flipped the phone over into the rocks, and then the video cut off.

Play stupid games; win stupid prizes.

So it looked like that one was indeed a bear attack. No help for me.

Knock! Knock! on the door startled me. And then the door opened.

"How's it going?" Kieron asked as he walked in and sat down in one of the uncomfortable wooden chairs.

"Not great yet," I admitted. "What're you up to?"

"Downloading the next batch of security footage. Figured I'd come check on you. What did you think of the videos I sent?"

"I wish we had found the smoking gun—or a shambling zombie. But there were some interesting bits. That cheerleader, Tiffani-Amber, she seemed really to hesitate when she saw Ms. Pruett. And then where was that other kid going so early in the morning in the school?"

"And did you see Douche Bag?"

"Yeah! That was a surprise. I had no idea he was here. Just one more thing to worry about now. What if he recognizes us? I ran into him in the hallway a few minutes ago. He was all – *Don't I know you*. Yeah, we're going to be scrambling if he remembers us."

"Well, I don't think I have to worry about him remembering me. Don't you remember? He called me Kevin my entire freshman year."

I laughed. I had forgotten that. I called Kieron "Kevin" as a joke for most of that year too. He hated it.

"Yeah, I didn't play football, so I was just a body in a seat in his class. But, to be safe, I think we should stay away from his classroom."

"He's not a teacher," I said seriously.

"What? Really?"

"Yeah, he's Dean of Students. His office is actually right next to this one."

"Crap. Really?"

"Yup. I got the warning not to get too comfortable, because the principal's office here was going to be his soon."

"Ugh. I can't think of anything worse than him being a dean than him being principal." Kieron shook his head in disbelief.

"Betsy thinks it's a long shot. She says there are quite a few people interested in the position that have been here for years."

"Thank God! Douche Bag definitely doesn't need any more power."

The three-minute warning bell sounded, indicating school was about to start.

"Well, I better get back at it. Anything else I can help you with?" Kieron said as he stood up.

"Actually, can you look into Thomas Evanson's school record? And, while you're at it, might as well check out Tiffani-Amber Blair."

"Got it, boss," Kieron snapped a salute and turned and walked out.

Chapter 8

Shortly after the final bell rang signaling the start of the first period, there was another knock on the door.

"Come in," I called out, closing the notes I had been making on my laptop.

It was Betsy, with Tiffani-Amber sullenly following behind. I stood up from my chair.

"This is Tiffani-Amber," Betsy said obviously. "I've called Thomas down as well for you. I'll have him wait in the reception area, if he shows up. It sometimes takes a couple of calls to get him to come down."

"Thanks, Betsy. I appreciate it."

"Tiffani-Amber, please have a seat," I said motioning to the chairs as I sat down.

Tiffani-Amber had the little chic backpack I had seen in the security video, but today she was dressed in a pink and blue plaid schoolgirl skirt, a fluffy pink sweater, and knee-high white boots. She reminded me of that old video of Britney Spears. She even had her hair in two ponytails—a look I could never, ever, ever pull off. Her skin was sun-kissed, and I wondered if it was left over from lounging in the summer sun or if it was spray-on. As she sat down and tilted her head at me, I was overwhelmed with the scent of her perfume.

It was strong.

And I recognized it.

And it was my favorite. Armani—Acqua d'Amore. I hated her just a little for wearing it.

"I'm Ms. Harris. I work for the school district, and I'm doing a report on Ms. Pruett's accident."

She crossed her legs and leaned back arrogantly in her chair as I pulled out a paper notebook and turned to a blank page. Can a person lean in a chair arrogantly? Yup, she did it—quite well in fact.

"Tiffani-Amber. That's a pretty name." I knew too many girls like her. Perfect make up. Perfect hair. Perfectly coordinated outfit. A little flattery could soften her up a bit. Let her know I wasn't a threat.

"Thanks," she said obviously used to hearing compliments. "My mom was a *Saved by the Bell — 90210 —* Tiffani-Amber Theissen fan growing up, so she named me after her. So why am I here? I really have more important things to do than talk about my name."

OK… so that didn't work so well.

I cleared my throat. "I understand you found Ms. Pruett Wednesday morning. Can you tell me what happened exactly? Start from the beginning, please."

Tiffani-Amber sighed heavily. "I already told the police and Mr. Stevens what happened. I don't know why I have to keep repeating myself."

"Humor me," I said and gave her my best glare.

To her credit, she held my eye contact much longer than most nons. I had been taught this glare by an Alp, on a trip my mom and I took to Germany a few years ago. I knew it was intimidating and made the person I was glaring at very uncomfortable. There was no better glare when I really put my mind to it. In fact, most people couldn't last more than three seconds without looking away.

"Fine," she said as she broke eye contact with me

finally. "I got to school Wednesday and parked outside C door, like normal. When I got out of my car, I saw Ms. Pruett on the steps. I ran over to her. The janitor was there. I told him to go get help, and I'd call 911."

I pretended to take notes as Tiffani-Amber spoke.

"It took the ambulance forever to get there, and I ruined my Burberry cashmere scarf trying to stop the woman from bleeding to death."

I wondered if she saw my eye roll.

"Thank you. What were you doing at school so early?" I asked. I watched her facial expression to see if I could detect any dishonesty.

"We have cheer practice in the mornings twice a week. I have to be there even earlier to prep for it."

There was a little lift of the eyebrow. Was that not quite true?

"You mentioned the janitor was there."

"Yeah. At first I didn't see him. He's short. And he was over on the other side of the stairs. He was holding on to Ms. Pruett's hand. He obviously was trying to stop the bleeding too."

"And then he went to get help," I prompted, "but he went to the next door down. Do you know why?"

"No idea," Tiffani-Amber said simply. "Maybe he didn't want to climb around Ms. Pruett?"

That was possible.

"Did you see anyone else around? Any animals? Hear anything?"

"No. Of course, I was pretty much out of my car and immediately helping Ms. Pruett, so it wasn't like I was really looking around."

Another subtle lift of her perfectly arched eyebrows, and I knew it was a lie. I scribbled random notes on the pad to keep up the charade.

"Mr. Stevens mentioned you left as soon as the ambulance arrived. Where did you go?"

"Umm," she replied snootily as if I just asked the stupidest question on the face of the planet, "I had to change and get my clothes to the cleaners ASAP. It was bad enough my scarf was ruined—would you believe the EMT tried to give it back to me when they got there? Eww!" she said in disgusted disbelief.

"Yeah, EMTs. What was he thinking?" Was this girl really this shallow?

"Right?! So my scarf was trashed, I wasn't going to ruin more of my clothes. I had blood on my jacket and my slacks. And Mr. Wu—my dry cleaner—said the jacket was going to be fine, but he wasn't sure about my slacks. They're wool. And I still have no idea if they're going to survive," she ended forlornly.

"I literally just got them last weekend, when we popped over to the city for the weekend."

"Chicago?" I asked.

"Uh no. New York." She sighed an exasperated at my idiocy sigh and continued. "Anyway, the slacks fit me like a glove, and I'm so hard to fit properly, because I'm, you know, athletic but petite."

"We all have our crosses to bear."

"And these slacks. Oh! You should feel them! So soft! Plus, they're part of Sebastian's Finter collection, so I just *had* to have them."

I knew I was going to regret asking, but I just couldn't help myself… "Finter?"

Tiffani-Amber cocked her head at me and smiled as if I'd just said something amusing, "Fall – winter – finter. I'm sure you've read about…" I watched her eyes flash to the simple button down top and yellow jacket I was wearing. "Oh… or maybe you haven't"

Her smile turned cruel.

I wanted to punch her in the throat.

"Anyway, they were really nice slacks, and now I have no idea if I'll ever get to wear them again. And, worse, no one even had a chance to see me in them!"

"That must be very traumatic for you," I said with more than an ounce of sarcasm in my voice. "What is the janitor's name that was helping you with Ms. Pruett?" I needed to change the subject. Maybe she could at least be helpful with that.

"How would I know?" she said furrowing her eyebrows at me.

Guess not.

"It was that janitor that doesn't speak English in the morning," she added.

OK, I knew what she meant, but sometimes my verbal filter goes on the fritz, especially when someone is frustrating me. "So does he speak English in the afternoons?"

See. Me. Smart ass.

"Yeah."

Wait… what?!

I looked across the desk at her, and she was serious. But I had to clarify. "So… you're saying there's a janitor here that doesn't speak English in the mornings, but in the afternoon he does?"

"Yeah, it's so annoying!" Tiffani-Amber confirmed.

"Ummm… ok." What more could I say? "I appreciate your time. If you think of anything else, no matter how small or silly you think it might be, please come back and see me. OK?"

"Yeah, sure," she said as she stood up to go. She wouldn't come back. I knew it. A moment later she was out the door in a cloud of Armani.

I slumped back into my chair, leaned my head back

and tilted my head to the heavens. The ceiling was a dropped ceiling with acoustical tiles. I wish I had some pencils to throw up into it, to see if I could get them to stick.

Before I had a chance to sit up and open the desk drawer to see if the last occupant left any lead-filled darts for me to play with, the phone intercom buzzed. I pushed four buttons before I finally got it right.

"Yes?" I said, unsure how to answer.

"Ms. Harris?" Betsy's disembodied voice crackled through the speaker. "Thomas Evanson is here. Should I bring him to you now?"

"Yes, please," I replied. "Thanks."

A couple of minutes later, Betsy knocked on my door.

"Come in, Betsy," I called out.

"This is Thomas Evanson," Betsy AKA Captain Obvious, said as she firmly guided the kid I had seen in the clip through the doorway.

Thomas was wearing the same, oversized jacket, a t-shirt and baggy jeans. He was short—at least a couple of inches shorter than me. His hair was lank and in his eyes, and it looked like he hadn't washed it in a few days. I was pretty sure this kid wasn't going to smell of designer cologne.

"Thanks, Betsy," I said to send her on her way. Thomas stayed standing at the doorway, as if at any moment he was going to bolt.

"Thomas," I started. "Do you go by Thomas or Tom?"

"It's whatever," he said and focused on the floor in front of him.

"OK, Thomas then. Come sit down, please."

He sighed and slunk forward. When he reached the

84

chair, he slumped into it, eyes downward.

"Thanks," I said. This was going to be tough. I could feel his defensiveness rolling off him in waves. I had to be careful, or this would be a complete waste of time. "My name is Ms. Harris. I'm with the school district and doing a report on Ms. Pruett's accident Wednesday."

That got a reaction.

Instantly he looked up at me, flipping his hair out of his eyes with a flick of his head. Startling bright green eyes glared intensely at me.

"What?! Because I was on campus I had something to do with it?! This is bullshit!" he spat not taking his eyes from mine. Whoa. Maybe he'd taken lessons from an Alp.

With his hair out of his face, I could see how gaunt this kid was. A glance down showed his collarbones peeking out under his gray t-shirt, at the opening of the too big jacket. His skin tone was sallow. And he had purplish rings under his eyes betraying obvious lack of quality sleep.

My heart went out to the kid.

"No, no, no," I quickly reassured him. "I just want to see if maybe you saw something others didn't see. You're good."

He narrowed his eyes at me, skeptical.

"So why were you at school so early Wednesday morning?" I asked hopefully innocently enough.

"Oh, sure!" he snapped. "I'm good, but now you're accusing me of not having a reason to be at school at that time? Every time something goes wrong, this school blames it on me! Just suspend me or whatever and get it over with. It's not like I haven't been through this before."

His hair had fallen back into his eyes. It shielded him behind a dark curtain. He didn't do anything to fix it.

Crap. This wasn't going well.

"I'm sorry," I said gently. "I was just curious. I'm sure

you had a perfectly good reason for being here." And I'd do some digging and figure out why, just in case this was all a smoke screen. "Can you tell me, did you see anything unusual Wednesday morning? Anyone acting strangely? Any animals? Anything at all? I really am sorry, Thomas, that that came out wrong, and I made you feel like I was accusing you of something."

I was sincere. I had a feeling this kid had bigger problems than zombies to worry about.

He flipped his bangs out of his eyes again and studied me.

"Tom. It's Tom," he finally said.

"Tom. Thanks," I replied.

"Nah," he said dismissively. "Thanks for saying you're sorry. No one ever does that."

"That sucks." What else could I say?

"Yeah, it's whatever."

"It's not whatever. You probably know that." This time I held his gaze. He acknowledged it with an almost imperceptible head nod.

"I really didn't see anything, until the ambulance was there." His tone was sincere. I believed him.

"You saw the ambulance?" I prodded.

"Yeah. I was over in the D hall, first floor and heard something. I went and looked out the door and saw them pulling up."

"Were you able to see Ms. Pruett from the door?"

"Yeah. Kind of. I saw Tiffani-Amber crouched over her and holding Ms. Pruett's hand wrapped in something. It looked like there was a lot of blood. I… I…" he trailed off and turned back to looking at the floor.

"It's OK, Tom," I reassured him.

He took a moment, and I waited.

"I had to go throw up," he said super-quietly, head

still down.

Instincts took over, and I came around the desk and crouched down in front of him. I put my hand on his shoulder and felt the boniness under his jacket.

"Hey," I said bending my head down to try to see into his eyes. "It's OK. I would've barfed too." I wouldn't have. I've seen so much worse. But a little white lie wouldn't hurt.

"Really?" he asked hopefully, bringing his head up a little.

"Absolutely! I get nauseous if my burger isn't cooked all the way through." Another white lie. I loved my burgers just this side of mooing.

"Me too," he said and, for the first time, I saw a flicker of a smile.

I stood up and sat on the edge of the desk, keeping our interaction informal and staying close. "Did you happen to see the janitor that helped Tiffani-Amber?"

"Yeah. Tiffani-Amber was yelling at him to get help. But he doesn't speak English. I was going to say something, but then he turned around and... well... there was just so much blood... that's when I had to run to the bathroom."

"Totally understandable. Do you know the janitor's name?"

"Of course. That's Alejandro. He's the only good person working here. I think he likes me because I speak Spanish with him. Most of the other kids don't bother to speak to him, since he doesn't speak English."

"Tiffani-Amber said something about him only speaking Spanish in the morning, but he speaks English in the afternoon. What's that about?" I had to ask.

Tom started laughing. It was an honest, full-bellied laugh. It was nice to hear and even brought a little color into his cheeks.

"She's an idiot. That is hilarious. Of course she'd

think that," he said through the laughter. "That's Izzy." He continued to laugh.

"So Izzy speaks Spanish in the morning and English in the afternoon?" I was so confused.

"No, no, no," Tom said as he caught his breath. "Alejandro and Izzy are twins. They're both from Mexico. Alejandro works the late night into the morning shift. Izzy works during school hours. Izzy speaks pretty good English. Alejandro really doesn't." He shook his head in disbelief. "I can't believe she thought they were the same dude! They even wear different colors. Alejandro always wears orange. Izzy always wears blue. You'd think the fashion princess would've at least noticed that."

That made so much more sense. And now I had the name of the janitor that was obviously the first one to see Ms. Pruett. Maybe he'd have more info for me. This could be the lead I was looking for.

"I need to speak to Alejandro. But my Espanol es no bueno. Do you speak Spanish well? Could you help me translate?"

"Yeah, I'm pretty fluent," Tom said sitting up a little straighter. "But Alejandro took time off starting today."

"Really? That's inconvenient," I said, and the air quickly deflated from my sails.

"Well, he wanted to go visit his family in Mexico. And, well, he has cancer so was worried he wouldn't make it to winter break."

"That's horrible," I said sincerely. Cancer sucks, no matter who's affected—even a stranger. A said a quick mental prayer for the poor guy. No wonder he looked so awful in the video. "Well, I'm glad he's going to see his family. Do you know when he's going to be back?" It was a long shot, but it seemed like Tom and Alejandro were buds.

"A couple of weeks. I can help you talk to him then,

if you'd like."

"OK, thanks. I appreciate it," I said and moved back around the desk to sit in my chair. A couple of weeks? If I didn't have this case wrapped up by then, Elmview was going to be the epicenter of a zombie pandemic. "I really do thank you for your help. If you think of anything else, please come see me."

"Oh OK," Tom said obviously not happy our conversation was over. That was sad that talking to me might be the highlight of this kid's day. He stood and started to walk to the door.

"Tom," I called out, and once again came around the desk, "if you ever need anything…" I handed him my card. It was just my phone number. No name. Nothing else. "… call me. OK? Anything."

He flipped his hair out of his eyes and smiled slightly at me. "Thanks. I'm fine. But… thanks." With that, he stuck the card in his back pocket and left the office.

I didn't know what the deal was with that kid, but I said a little prayer for him too.

Chapter 9

The rest of the morning had me staring at the notes in my computer utterly confused. One zombie attack. No leads. No one saw anything unusual. I started to question whether or not it really was a zombie attack. Why hadn't there been any other attacks in over 48 hours? That wasn't very zombie-like. Was it really just a random coyote bite?

I knew better. I saw the spread of the infection.

There was simply something else I was missing.

A knock on the door startled me. Kieron entered and thankfully interrupted my musing. Maybe he had something.

"What's up?" I asked hopefully.

Kieron said nothing and crossed the room. He came around to my side of the desk. I looked up at him confused, as he walked behind me and then leaned over my left shoulder. I could feel the heat of his body as he bent over me. His right hand braced himself on the back of my chair and his left hand opened a program on my computer. I could smell the clean scent of him—body wash and fabric softener. I admit, I turned a little more toward him and inhaled deeply, hoping he wouldn't notice as he typed something on my keyboard. Why did he smell so good lately even now without cologne on?

The traitorous butterflies started fluttering around in my stomach, and I could feel the heat rising in response in my skin. His chest was right there. A triangle of skin was exposed from where his shirt had gapped open. I could just barely see the top of his pec. His skin was still lightly tanned from the summer, and it contrasted against the white, crispness of his button down shirt.

Kieron turned his attention to me and caught me gazing longingly at his chest.

Ugh. Why was that lust bag still affecting me?

"Check this out," Kieron said.

Check out his chest? Doing that.

No. Computer. Seriously, Jenna, focus! I forced my head to turn to my laptop screen.

Kieron had pulled up Tom's transcript for the last three years. Hmm… I would not have guessed he was a junior. I had thought he was a freshman. Interesting.

Tom's transcript showed a decent Bs and Cs student freshman year and then a quick decline starting at the beginning of his sophomore year. So far, the first two months of junior year had been the worst ever. He was currently failing 4 classes—Algebra 2, Chemistry, Spanish 2, and… Ms. Pruett's Sophomore English he was repeating after failing the same class last year.

"So he probably wasn't a fan of Ms. Pruett," I surmised.

"It gets more interesting,"

Kieron clicked the screen to show more of Tom's transcript. Since the beginning of last school year, Tom had been suspended three times. The first was for throwing a book at Ms. Pruett at the beginning of last year. The second was for getting into an altercation with one of the lunch ladies. The most recent was just last month for setting a fire in the chemistry lab.

"Wow. I sensed the kid was having a hard time, but this *is* interesting."

Kieron typed quickly into the school's records system he had gained access to—I wondered with or without permission—and this time Tiffani-Amber's transcript popped up. I took over control and scrolled through. She was a solid C student for her first three years at South, with a smattering of As in Freshmen PE, Drawing 1 and, surprisingly, Home Economics. However, this semester, she was also experiencing some trouble. She had a D- in two classes—Statistics and Composition… taught by none other than Ms. Pruett. She wasn't failing, but I'm sure the D- in those classes might be threatening her status to cheer.

"Hmmm…" I said trying to process this new information. "So both Tom and Tiffani-Amber aren't doing well with Ms. Pruett's class. And Tom's had some… ummm… behavior issues. This still doesn't make sense. What do you think?"

I looked up as Kieron turned his gaze to mine. He could very easily lean in and kiss me again, and I wouldn't complain. Nope. Not one little bit. But just as I thought he may do just that, Kieron stood up, and I immediately noticed his lack of nearness.

He ran his hand through his hair and narrowed his eyes in thought. "I have no idea. Even if they both have a motive to want Ms. Pruett harmed, neither of them are zombies, obviously."

"Although maybe that's why Tiffani-Amber wears so much perfume," I snarked.

"Well, I'm going to go back to staring at security videos from sporadic camera angles," Kieron said with a disgruntled sigh as he made his way toward the door. "Let me know if you need anything."

"Will do. And let me know if you find anything else."

Chapter 10

I spent the next couple of hours staring at my laptop. I read every bit of information in both Tom's and Tiffani-Amber's electronic file. The bell rang, and my stomach gave a rumble. Pavlovian, it must be third lunch. I texted Kieron.

Are you hungry?

His reply came quickly.

Nah. Had a bag of Cheetos. I think I might be on to something. Got about 30 min more vid to watch. Text u when done.

That sounded promising. My stomach gave another grumble and ordered me to find food. I headed quickly to the cafetorium. The large central space was filled with over 100 round tables, each with eight attached stools radiating out from the base of the table. *Spiders within the spider* was my immediate thought.

The area was accented with Halloween decorations. Pennants of orange and black with H-A-P-P-Y H-A-L-L-O-W-E-E-N hung across two edges of the cafetorium about fifteen feet up. Papier mâché jack-o-lanterns hung down at intervals from those. They were low enough I was sure some of the guys could probably jump up and hit them. They all looked pristine, so either Elmview South had better behaved guys than North, or these were new decorations. Scarecrows stuck into hay bales were placed sporadically around the cafetorium. They seemed to be looming over the dining students and were far more creepy than if they had been ghosts are something else traditionally scary.

On each table were orange table topper signs. I couldn't read the full details as I walked by, but they seemed to be reminding the students about a Halloween dance tonight.

Some students jostled for places in line to the food stations positioned at the back of the ginormous space, where the school kitchens were located. Other students eagerly took seats with their friends. Some wandered about finding being social more important than eating. Others still filtered in slowly from the hallways, clearly not in a rush to get to their lunch.

The cafetorium smelled of food and teenage desperation as I stood back and watched the social hierarchy play out before me. A tale as old as time, clusters of tables were clearly the property of certain social groups. I could see the tables with the jocks. Most of the guys were wearing letter jackets, despite the fact they were inside and it was rather warm in the cafetorium. There was a nearby group of tables with really well-dressed kids. They looked like they should be in a movie about a high school, not actually going to high school. They all had brought their lunch, and I noticed several were pulling out spreads of sushi and sashimi from stainless steel small coolers with YETI emblazoned on the side. There was a small cluster of tables that must be the band kids' turf. I only surmised this based on the fact that several of the kids had their instrument with them. Other tables were clearly marked for outcasts. I scanned the tables for the only two students I knew in the school and found neither. They must have a different lunch.

It was loud in the cafetorium. Cacophonous. Was that a word? If not, it should be because that's what this was. Our cafeteria space at North was smaller and only two stories and was not nearly this loud. One thousand-plus teenagers hungry and happy to not be behind a desk made a lot of noise.

I made my way to the salad bar area of the food stations in the kitchen area. This was a luxury we didn't have at North. I was definitely jealous of this. I filled an ecologically-friendly paper to-go container with baby spinach, red peppers, tomatoes, and some grilled chicken. I drizzled it with Cesar dressing and topped it with a good portion of shredded Parmesan and croutons. I crossed to a cashier and paid my salad weight. Stuck to the side of the cash register was a poster also promoting the dance. While I waited for the cashier to run my card, I took a closer look.

> Zombies for Everyone!
> Come dance until you're undead!
> Friday, October 21st
> 7 pm – 10 pm
> Prizes for best zombie costumes!
> Scariest – Funniest – Best Zombie Famous Person – Best Zombie Couple
> $15 per person - $25 per couple
> Tickets available in home room from Student Council members

Really? A zombie dance. The universe just enjoyed screwing with me sometimes.

I stood at the periphery of the tables, with my box of salad, and felt like the new kid at school. Should I sit with some of the students? There were a couple of tables that only had three or four students, plenty of room for a pretend school district employee.

Nope. That would be awkward.

I could go back to my temporary office and stare at my laptop screen a bit more. But I really needed a break—clear the cobwebs out and get a fresh set of eyes on the case. Maybe I'd just find a quiet spot down one of the hallways to sit by myself and eat.

That sounded like a plan.

I headed off to the nearest hallway to my right. It was much like halls at North. Rows of lockers were broken up by the occasional door to a classroom. Looking at the numbers on the lockers, I was clearly in the F corridor. The further I traveled down the long hall, the quieter it got. It was a welcome relief from the noise of the cafetorium.

Halfway down the corridor was a stairwell doorway with a number combo lock. We had similar stairwell doors at North. The locks prevented students from using these stairwells. As a freshmen, we used to be able to use these stairs, but the slightly hidden nature of them meant they were perfect places for students to get up to trouble. Minor offenses, such as using the stairwells for make-out sessions, all the way to criminal offenses like drug deals were happening out of the direct sight of teachers and administration. By the start of sophomore year, these stairwells were locked and only teachers were allowed to use them to quickly go from one floor to the next, without the crush of students they normally had to face on the normal staircases. It looked like South had adopted a similar position.

The door was a smooth surface to lean against and one that wouldn't be opening unexpectedly before the bell rang…

… or so I thought.

The door swung open nearly smacking me in the face. Thankful for quick reflexes, I grabbed it just before it had a chance to break my nose and knock my lunch from my hands. Tom stumbled partially out of it, looking slightly green and frightened. I pulled the door open fully and grabbed ahold of him.

"Tom! Are you OK?" It was dumb question. He clearly was not. So I clarified, "What's wrong?"

"Ms. Harris! It's... Mr. Briggs...he's... I don't know... but there was blood... and something... I think it went on the roof."

Crap. I couldn't let him leave if this was a zombie attack.

"It's OK, Tom. I need you to do me a big favor."

"OK," he said hesitatingly. He looked so young.

"I want you to sit inside here, in front of the door—"

"I—" he began to protest.

"You don't have to go any further than right here on the floor. OK? I just need you to be here so if I get hurt, you can call 911. OK? Can you do that for me?"

"Yeah... I guess. If I just have to sit here."

He moved into the stairwell, and I followed closing the door behind us.

"Did you eat lunch?" I asked

"Nah," he said studying the speckled flooring.

How was that possible. If this was his lunch period, he definitely should've already been in the cafetorium eating. So I had assumed he had first or second lunch. If that was the case, then why hadn't he already eaten? I remembered how bony his shoulder had felt and had a sneaking suspicion why he hadn't eaten.

"Here," I said and handed him my salad. "Eat lunch. Sit here. Wait for me. Got it?"

"Got it," he said. He sat down and opened the box of salad and immediately began to scarf it down.

"Thank you, Tom. Now I'll be right back. Please stay

put. Even if the bell rings. I'll write you a pass."

I sprinted up the stairs. Sure enough, on the first half of the stair run going from the third floor to the roof was a sprawled body—a man I assumed was Mr. Briggs. The sleeve of his right arm was soaked completely in blood, and a pool of it was starting to trickle down the steps and pool on the landing. Mr. Briggs' eyes were open but rolled up into his head and his mahogany-colored skin was beginning to pale with blood loss.

Crap. There was only one thing I could do.

Call for help.

I hated to call for help on a private case like this. OK, I hated calling for help on any case. I always felt like I should be able to handle things on my own. The question that always haunted me was—would Mom have called for help? I'll admit, it tweaked at my ego a bit. But this injury needed stabilization before I could even treat the bite, and that was outside my wheelhouse.

I dialed the Consortium's emergency support number as I stepped to the corner of the third floor landing. The video call connected immediately.

"CES," a middle-aged woman with nearly translucent skin, pursed coral lips and jet-black hair cut into a short bob answered curtly.

"I have a Code 42. Jenna Sutton. 1-0-foxtrot-2-tango-1-6-9-whiskey," I responded and flipped my video to the forward camera to show the stairwell landing. "Clear to receive."

"One moment."

The woman's face disappeared and the screen went to black with the word "HOLD" in white lettering across it. A moment later, the air in front of me shimmered and rippled, like the air immediately above a black asphalt road on a hot summer day. A flash of light made me squint my eyes closed.

And then they were there. Three men. Two of them I had seen in passing and on other jobs, but I only knew them by sight. One I definitely knew.

Colm McAleer.

Colm was an Irish-born warlock I had worked with several times over the last year. He headed up one of the clean-up crews for the Consortium. His and his team's job was to help Hunters and other non-magical Consortium employees when needed. His job varied from helping capture an unruly supe to literally cleaning up a physical supernatural mess. As this wasn't an official Consortium case, his presence was going to cost me a lot of money. I hoped the school district wouldn't balk at the cost. It *was* listed in the contract, but I'm sure Pringle didn't fully read the contract. No one ever did.

Colm was, for lack of a better word, ridiculously handsome. Like he was so good-looking I could look at him all day long and never get bored. His hair was a warm, dark cinnamon color, and it was highlighted with copper. It was clipped short on the sides, but the top was left long enough to artfully spike. He had a strong jaw that was often hidden by start of a neatly-kept beard. Between the hair and the beard, I was pretty sure he spent more time getting ready in the morning than I did.

However long it took, it was worth it.

His skin was fair, like so many of his countrymen, and he had a very light smattering of freckles across the bridge of his nose. His freckles were so light I didn't notice them until the third time we had worked together, and I had been thrown into him, courtesy of a Skunk Ape. I ended up gazing up into his face from mere inches. It was that encounter that also helped me realize his eyes weren't just brown, but rather brown with olive flecks and ringed with a dark green.

And when he spoke… oh…my…God. His accent was totally swoon-worthy! It was like chocolate for the ears. Sometimes I couldn't understand what he was saying. I never was quite sure if it was his accent or if he was just throwing Irish words in here and there. But either way, it didn't matter. Colm could read the phone book to me, and I would listen to him for hours on end.

I had no idea how old Colm was, which was a bit of a problem. Witches and warlocks aged slower than humans once they hit their 20s. So although he appeared to be in his young 20s, he could easily be 30 or even 60 years old. I hadn't found a way to tactfully ask him for sure—even with witches and warlocks age was a tender subject. I had once asked how long he'd been in the States, thinking that might give me a clue, but his answer of just four years didn't tell me much.

"Well 'ello, you," he said with a cheery smile when he saw me. "Aren't you an aisling in yellow."

"Thanks," I said. I wasn't sure what an 'aisling' was, but the way he said it made me blush nonetheless. "It's good to see you too, Colm."

He looked up the stairwell and saw the sprawled and bleeding Mr. Briggs. "So what do we 'ave here?"

I gave him the details as quickly as possible, while he worked some healing magic on Briggs to ensure he didn't die before he could counter the zombie bite. One of his colleagues started sealing off the doorway on the third floor. The other went down to wipe Tom's memory and send him on his way.

The situation in the stairwell in hand, I sidestepped around Briggs body and headed for the rooftop door. Thankfully, there was no lock to the roof. I flew through the door and out on the roof. It was enormous. The sheer size of the school was almost boggling from this vantage point. Four stairwell entrances peaked out halfway down each of their respective legs of the school's spidery shape. Apparently the architect had only designed these extra staircases in every other corridor. Other than that, there was only a smattering of air handler units dotted across the body's roof and what appeared to be a storage shed.

I quickly made my way out to the main rooftop and starting checking around each of the air handler units. The rooftop itself was scattered with gravel, and it crunched beneath my feet as I went. No one would be able to sneak around up here. That was a bonus. I headed to the storage shed. It was a long shot, but maybe someone was hiding in there. But it too was locked with a combination lock keypad.

I went to the edge of the building and looked down at the parking lot very far below. There appeared to be no fire escapes or any other way to exit the roof, other than down one of the other stairwells. It was definitely too high for someone, even an already dead someone, to jump. If the zombie had instead escaped down one of the other three stairwells, it could be anywhere now. But if it was on the move, maybe Kieron would catch it on camera.

I pulled my cell phone from my pocket and called Kieron as I walked back to the F corridor stairwell to check on Colm and Mr. Briggs.

"Hey. We just had an attack in the stairwell going to the roof in Corridor F. I think the zombie crossed the roof and went down another stairwell. Can you check the cameras going in and out of the stairwell doors?"

"I'm on it," was his reply and then a click.

I went down the flight of stairs to find Colm squatting next to a shirtless Mr. Briggs. He had just finished applying salve to the three slices he had made in Brigg's arm above the bite mark that was now bared to the world. Smoke began to rise from the wound and filled the small, enclosed area with smoke that burned the back of my throat.

"Eww! What's that smell?!" someone coughed from above.

Instincts kicked in, and I turned and flew up the stairs to block whoever was coming in from the roof.

It was Tiffani-Amber.

Of course it was.

"Tiffani-Amber!" I said and I knew my voice was shrill. "What are you doing here?"

The smoke continued to rise and swirl around the two of us, luckily blocking the view down the stairs as the nosey cheerleader tried to peer around me to see its source. She had her hand over her nose and mouth and her face was wrinkled up in disgust. I didn't really blame her. The smell was awful— a combination of burnt microwave popcorn and scorched vacuum cleaner belt, with a hint of death. But in a few moments, it would be completely gone.

"I…" she started and then was interrupted by the bell. "I have to get to class," she finished as she tried to dodge around me.

"You can't go this way," I said sounding as authoritative as I possibly could. "Back up to the roof. Now."

I don't think people ever talked to her with the tone I used, because she just stood there confused and unsure of what to do.

"But I'm going to be—"

"Now!" I reiterated and pointed at the rooftop door as further direction. She turned and went back onto the roof as I followed her.

"Let's have a chat in my office," I said and steered her to the main roof area then the stairwell leading into the A corridors. She walked silently and sullenly in front of me. However, by the time we sat in my office and the door was closed behind us, she had regained her self-assured arrogance.

She flounced into the chair, her nose slightly raised at

me, and said, "I really need to get to class. Some of us have things to do around here."

Oh, I had things I wanted to do around here—one of them was to punch her in that snotty nose she was looking down at me from.

"Why don't you tell me what you were doing up on the roof, Ms. Blair," I said ignoring her snipe. "My understanding is those stairwells are for staff only, and certainly no students are allowed on the roof."

OK, that was a bit of a bluff. I didn't know that for 100 percent certain. But given the locked doors similar to South, it made me 90 percent sure that's how it was.

"I have permission," Tiffani-Amber said with a satisfied smirk.

"Really?" I replied unimpressed. I stood up and leaned across the desk in what I hoped was an intimidating manner. I held Tiffani-Amber's gaze and this time I saw her confidence falter just a bit. "Someone lit a fire in the stairwell. You seem to be an unauthorized student. You do the math."

OK another fib, but it seemed to work.

"Wait!" Now she looked actually concerned. Perfect. "You don't think I had anything to do with it, do you?"

"If I don't get some answers, you definitely will be the first person the police will be speaking with. So let's try this again. What were you doing on the roof? Who gave you the access code? I want all the details."

"I was just going to my next class," she said earnestly. "I have to go all the way from the end of C corridor to F corridor, but my locker's on the third floor of H, and since it's during a lunch period change, it's always really hard to get all the way from C to H and then over to F in time. Mr. Briggs gave me the code, so I wouldn't be late to his class."

She finished and looked at me expectantly. My Spidey Senses were telling me there was still something she was hiding.

"Actually, I found Mr. Briggs passed out in the stairwell from the smoke." Yup, more lies, but my gut was usually good at telling me what string to pull to unravel a person's truth. I also remembered her transcript. "You're not doing so well in his class, are you?"

"I'm doing…okay," she hedged; her eyes widened slightly with the implied accusation. "But what's that got to do with it?"

"Well, a teacher that supposedly has given you access to restricted stairwells is found unconscious in a stairwell that was set on fire. A teacher who just so happens to be from a class you're struggling in, right now during peak football cheer season. I assume Elmview South has GPA requirements for all of their athletes—including cheerleaders, correct?"

Oh that hit her. She saw the dominoes I was not-so-subtly setting up.

"He probably set the fire himself," she countered forcefully. "That's why he gave me the code. I caught him smoking in his classroom one morning, when I was supposed to come in for extra help, and he forgot. Smoking on campus is cause for immediate suspension—students and teachers alike. I… I…" she hesitated to continue. I waited silently, not letting her off the hook.

"I told him I'd tell Mrs. Cowell, that was our old principal, if he didn't give me the access code. I mean, it's so stupid! We could use those stairwells last year. But then the stupid dirtbags at North had trouble and somehow we got locked out of them too! I mean we're not like North!

"So he gave it to me. And, honestly, I was just coming from my locker. I didn't go into F stairwell, other than the two feet in when I saw you. You have to believe me!"

She seemed earnest. But then I'd been lied to by the

best. And the fact that she was at both Pruett's and Briggs's accident scenes was either a huge coincidence, or I really was on the track of something, albeit not a bit of arson.

"Who else was up on the roof when you were up there?"

"I didn't see anyone else."

OK that really sounded sincere. That didn't necessarily make a difference whether or not she had anything to do with the attacks. But she obviously wasn't a zombie. Her perfume was strong, but definitely not 'cover the smell of death' strong.

Maybe.

No. She definitely wasn't a zombie. Zombies didn't talk, let alone whine and complain. But why was she at both attacks? Did she really just have the most awful luck? Or was I missing something?

I suppose the good news was the zombie hadn't moved on to some other area. It hadn't headed for the subdivision so close by. That had been my biggest fear that it was out in the wild spreading. The other good news was it still must be on school premises, because a zombie couldn't just saunter on and off school grounds.

Could it?

I would hope their security was a little more thorough than that.

And then there was Tom. He too had been at both scenes of the crime. He also was failing both Ms. Pruett's and Mr. Briggs' classes. He had a track record of violence. But I didn't sense he was a bad kid. And, again, clearly not a zombie himself.

So what was the connection I was missing here?

"Did you see anyone else coming in or out of the other stairwell?" I guessed the answer, but had to ask.

"No. I swear. I didn't see anyone."

I waited to see what else she would say. When after a long two minutes she said nothing more, I excused her from my office. I had a mystery to solve that wasn't getting any easier.

"How is he?" I asked Colm who was checking the bite wound on Mr. Briggs. Briggs' body. Briggs was now being magically levitated on a stretcher instead of sprawled uncomfortably on the stairs. The stairs below him were clean of blood and Brigg's bloody shirt was gone completely, and his pants he was (thankfully) still wearing showed no signs of the gruesome scene only a short while earlier.

"He'll be grand, as soon as we git a bit more blood back into 'im. Don't you be worryin' yer pretty, wee head now." He said the last bit with a saucy wink at me, and I instantly felt my traitorous blood vessels start to make me blush again.

Darn it! Why did this guy affect me like this?! Umm… because he was gorgeous and had a sexy accent and was a flirt beyond measure. Duh.

"Did ye catch the beast that did this to 'im?"

"No. I'm hoping Kieron caught something on video. It was gone by the time I got to the roof."

"Ah," Colm said with a waggle of his eyebrows, "so you be datin' the young Kieron, are ya?"

"No," I said quickly—probably too quickly—"I'm not dating the young Kieron or the old Kieron or any Kieron, for that matter."

"Good," he said simply as he signaled for his colleagues to take Mr. Briggs up to the roof—I assumed to materialize him back to the Consortium to ensure he fully healed.

"Good?" OK I was confused. And in my confusion, the question spurted out of my mouth.

"Yeah, it wouldn't be very kindly of me to be askin' out another fella's girl now, would it?"

Wait. What?

"Uhhh… no. I suppose it wouldn't."

"Now," he said stepping closer to me.

He smelled like sunshine and rain swirled into one. It was like a sun shower on gorgeous grassy knoll. The kind that takes you by surprise and makes you laugh and twirl around in it.

I could once again see that light smattering of freckles dotted across his nose. They were so adorable. I wanted to smile, but my face seemed to be frozen. In fact, my whole body seemed to be frozen except my heart, which was hammering so loudly in my chest I knew he could hear it. "Perhaps ye would do me the honor of lettin' me buy you dinner tonight?"

"I… I…" I stammered. Tonight? Yes! But no. I had a zombie. I couldn't take time off for a dinner date, no matter how amazing his eyes were. No matter how much I wanted to lean up on my tiptoes and kiss those perfect lips. No, I just couldn't.

"I know a place," he said as he reached out and placed his hands on my upper arms. Every nerve ending in my body went on high alert. His hands were warm, and he touched me firmly but gently—showing his strength but also his reserve. "Went to it with some mates a few weeks ago. The craic was ninety."

Craic? Ninety? I didn't know what he was saying but if it meant he was going to keep touching me…

The buzz of my phone broke the spell.

Wait. Was it a spell? He was a warlock after all. No. He wouldn't do that. A guy that good looking wouldn't need to spell a girl to get a date. Would he?

"Hey, what do you have for me?" It was Kieron, and I was hopeful he had good news for me.

"Nothing on the stairwells. But I have something else you need to see. I'm heading to your office right now."

"OK, be there in a minute," I replied then ended the call.

"*A ghr á*," Colm said to me with a devilish smile on his face, as he reached out with a finger and stroked the side of my cheek. Instantly, I felt the thrill of his touch sing in my veins in response, and it made my breath catch "Go. Catch yer zombie, lass. You and I will talk later." And in a shimmer he was gone.

Chapter 11

"OK, tell me you have good news for me."

Kieron was already in my office. Wow, it didn't take long for me to really consider this 'my' office.

"You're going to have to see this to believe it," Kieron responded beckoning me around the desk. He graciously got out of the chair and let me sit down. Who says chivalry is dead? His laptop was open, and he reached around me to push play.

It was more security footage of one of the corridors. Students were walking through the halls—some clustered in small groups, others walking alone. All seemed to be in a hurry, and it quickly became apparent why as, like magic, the halls cleared. The bell must've rung.

Then Tiffani-Amber sauntered down the hall. She had her little backpack on and some books in her hand. She was in jeans and a button-down shirt with the sleeves rolled up just slightly. Her hair was loose and hung in near-perfect ringlets. She looked like she could've just walked off a page of a Ralph Lauren ad. She ducked into the restroom, then in just over a minute was back out and headed back down the hallway.

Before she exited the frame, Mr. Durban appeared and stopped her. He was saying something to her. She looked up at him, clutched her books to her chest and said something in response. More unheard conversation ensued. I wasn't sure what they were saying to one another, but it was definitely an argument. Douche Bag Durban held out his hand expectantly. Tiffani-Amber took a step back from him, and I could see her shaking her head, her long, sleek ponytail swaying back and forth in answer.

Wait a second.

I reached out and paused the video. Although Tiffani-Amber and Durban were now at the edge of the security camera's field of vision. There definitely was an issue going on. I scrolled the clip back, watching the cheerleader walk backward and closer to the camera, just to be sure.

Yup.

Somehow, in a matter of sixty-five seconds in the bathroom, Tiffani-Amber had changed out of jeans and shirt to her full cheerleader uniform. She had managed to take her hair from loose ringlets to a perfectly smooth and straight ponytail, complete with annoying cheerleader spirit bow. I can get dressed quickly. But this was… magic? It would take more than that amount of time just to warm up my straightener. How had she not only straightened her hair, put it up so neatly, but also completely changed her outfit? And where were her other clothes? And was her cheerleading outfit in the bathroom waiting? I looked up at Kieron who was smiling.

"Pretty neat trick, huh?" He reached forward and fast-forwarded back to Tiffani-Amber and Durban.

The video began to play again. Once again, Douche Bag stuck his hand out and Tiffani-Amber stepped away from him. Durban took a step toward her and said something that clearly Tiffani-Amber didn't like. She now shook her head more rapidly, in a no response. I could see Durban say something, shrug then turn around as if he were about to walk away. Tiffani-Amber responded with what looked like 'wait' and Douche Bag turned back toward her. Tiffani-Amber than slowly handed Durban the topmost book in her arms.

"Take a closer look at this," Kieron stopped at Tiffani-Amber handing him the book.

"What is he doing?" I asked squinting at the frame, trying to see details. I reached forward and zoomed in. They were too far away to really see anything much. Zooming in just pixelated the image making both Tiffani-Amber and Durban look like random squares of colors. I zoomed back out to the normal view. The situation just didn't make sense. "Why is he taking that book from her? She doesn't look happy about it."

"That's what I thought exactly." Kieron took control and went back to when Tiffani-Amber came out of the bathroom and was closer to the camera. As she turned, he paused it and then zoomed in on her left hand and the topmost book she was carrying—the book that Durban forced her to give to him.

"This looked kind of familiar to me," Kieron started, "but I figured you're the expert, so you tell me."

I thought he was right. I tried to zoom in more, but that was the best we were going to get. The book looked to be covered in leather with runes tooled around the perimeter of the front cover. Tiffani-Amber's hand and forearm covered the center of the cover, but it definitely could be…

A grimoire.

I was impressed Kieron had spotted it. To my knowledge, he'd only seen one once, when he helped me bring in a witch who was taking the Hansel and Gretel story quite literally. She had set up a little cottage made of actual gingerbread in Smithwick Woods, a small forest preserve— popular place for kids to ride their bikes on the trails—in the nearby town of Simons Grove. The cottage was accented with all sorts of candies, and you could smell the delicious sweet smell of it from hundreds of feet away. Seven kids had gone missing. We had captured the witch, by pretending to be unsuspecting children. Everything had gone smoothly, until Kieron almost picked up the witch's grimoire.

Grimoires were bound to their witch or warlock. You never touched one, unless the witch or warlock gave it to you personally. I had heard different versions of what would happen to you if you did. None of them were pleasant. All of them were deadly.

"What the honest heck?" is all I could say as the pieces began to fall into place.

Guess it was time to talk to my favorite person—again.

"It's so good to hear from you," Aunt Cassie's voice came cheerfully through the phone. "Such a surprise though." Something in her tone made me think it was anything but a surprise to her.

"Hi, Aunt Cassie," I began. "I need your help with something."

I quickly explained the situation. I, obviously, couldn't accuse Tiffani-Amber of being a witch, let alone a Necromancer who raised the dead, on just a somewhat inconclusive and definitely grainy security camera video clip. If Cassandra would confirm Tiffani-Amber was definitely in her regional coven, then that would be the nail in the coffin.

"Hmmm…" Aunt Cassie's said with what came across as mock thoughtfulness. "This is a bit of a dilemma. I want to help you. I do. I truly do." That almost sounded sincere. "But…" There was always a 'but.' "Coven members are bound not to speak and reveal other coven members. You can understand that; I'm sure. It's a security measure."

I sighed. "Yeah, that makes sense. I just really don't want to end up bringing in a clean up team just to wipe her memory when she's a mortal, and I've accused her not only of being a witch but also raising a zombie. You know?"

"Hmmm…" More thoughtfulness, but this time it seemed for real. "Well, I wish I could help you, but our rules have been created for a reason. I'm so sorry.

"By the way, I'm going to be doing a little clean up of my hard drive in a few minutes. I need to move some of my photos off onto the cloud. I know there are some nice ones of your mother and I when we were younger that you'd love to see. I'll put them in a folder and share it with you. Be sure to check them out."

And then the phone went dead.

"Well, that was helpful. Not."

Way to change the subject and leave me hanging. Maybe she was still upset I hadn't let her know I was going to be in Chicago. Maybe I should've had coffee with her before we left the city. She probably thought I was trying to avoid her—she wouldn't be wrong—one day and then asking for a favor the next. Not a surprise she turned me away.

"Did she say she was going to share photos with you?" Kieron asked. Obviously I needed to turn down the call volume on my phone.

"Yeah. Some of my mom and her, she said. I knew there were rules about coven members revealing other members' names, but I was hoping she'd maybe be able to give me at least a 'yes' or 'no' about Tiffani-Amber."

"Do you even know how many members are in the coven?"

"A primary coven is no more than seven members, with seven being the ideal. However, there are then regional covens. Regional covens are compromised of up to 111 primary covens, so up to 777 members. They're based solely on geographic areas. Once a regional coven is filled in an area and a new primary coven is formed, six of the primary covens in the closest regional coven break off and form a new regional coven with the new primary coven.

"There's only one regional coven in the western Chicago area—that's the one Cassandra's in— so it must be less than 777 members. But I also heard talk that it's getting ready to split. So I bet it's in the upper end of the limit."

"So," Kieron replied, "maybe she just didn't immediately know if Tiffani-Amber is in the coven. So she couldn't give you that 'yes' or 'no' answer. You know?"

"I don't know. She's really on top of her members. She wants to be High Priestess for the US, and that—from what I hear—is almost purely a popularity contest in the end. I'd think—"

My phone vibrated with an e-mail notification interrupting what 'I thought.' Speak of the devil. It was Cassandra. More specifically, it was a notification that a new secure folder had been shared with me. I showed it to Kieron.

"Wow. That was fast," he noted. "Let's look at the pictures."

I wanted to argue that we didn't have time to look at old photos. We had a zombie on the loose and a possible rogue witch in our midst. It really wasn't time to go down memory lane. However, I still wasn't sure about Tiffani-Amber. If I accused her of being a witch and she wasn't, that was going to be a nightmare. *Although it might mean Colm would be back, and that wouldn't be a bad thing,* a little voice whispered in my head. I shook my head 'no.' I did not need more Colm distractions right now, no matter how hot those distractions were.

Without even thinking, I had opened the link to the

shared photos. Guess we were going to look at them. *Quickly though*, I promised myself.

The folder opened in list view. File names, sizes, dates, and file type were neatly listed. There were hundreds of photos in the folder. Cassandra must've already been uploading these when I called. Unless there was magic involved, which there likely was.

I scrolled through the file list. Each file was a series of numbers no indication of what the photo was. However, as I continued to scroll, I saw one outlier. It was a PDF file, not a JPG like all the others. I continued to scroll. Nope. Just one random PDF file. I double clicked it open.

It was a newsletter. Not just any newsletter—the *Western Chicago Regional Coven Weekly*. It was dated July 1st—so a few months ago. I wasn't sure why Aunt Cassie would've sent this to me, but perhaps there was a members list or something, which would be helpful. The front page featured a news story about two witches and a warlock who had been excommunicated from the regional coven at the last meeting. There was a photo of the three standing in a room with the coven members sitting in rings around them. The photo wasn't the greatest, since it had been taken from so far away, but it was easy to see that neither of the two women were Tiffani-Amber, so I moved on.

The next page had a listing of upcoming events for the remainder of the year. There was an article about preserving hard-to-find ingredients. Who knew yak's tears were a rare commodity and so hard to keep fresh? There was also a smattering of advertisements. But it was page three that had what I was looking for.

Page three featured a welcome to the newest members of the regional coven—all of who had been inducted on the summer solstice on June 20th. Twelve witches and warlocks stood in long white robes. Each person wore a unique botanical crown. Some had mostly leaves with berries and pinecones. Others' headpieces were primarily flowers. And there, in the middle of the group, front and center, was Tiffani-Amber, her head was encircled with a riot of blue bonnets and magnolia flowers, with trails of honeysuckles contrasting at her temples.

She was looking directly into the camera. Her chin angled slightly up, so she was peering down her nose just a bit at anyone who looked at the photo. Haughty—that was a word my mother would've used to describe the look. She wasn't smiling, none of the group was, but Tiffani-Amber definitely looked pleased with herself.

"So she's a witch?" Kieron asked incredulously.

"Looks that way. And it looks like it definitely was a grimoire she had. And I knew what I needed to do next."

Chapter 12

Tiffani-Amber looked pissed. There was no other word for it. She had full-on resting bitch face as she stared across the desk at me. I still couldn't believe this was who was controlling the zombie. Was she some sort of witchy prodigy? I mean, she'd only been inducted into the coven four months ago. I had always been led to believe raising a zombie took a lot of magic and a lot of training.

Now, how was I going to get her to admit to it and, more importantly, get her to de-animate the zombie?

"I know about the book," I started off small.

"Listen," she said narrowing her eyes and pursing her perfectly painted lips at me, "I actually do have classes I need to go to. I didn't start the fire. You know that. And I have no idea what book you're talking about. So," she continued as she stood up in a huff, put her little backpack on, and began to walk to the door, "if you have nothing else, I'm going back to class."

"I know about your grimoire," I clarified.

That stopped her in her tracks.

"My what?" she said turning to look at me cautiously.

"Your grimoire. The one you received on the summer solstice." I said it so matter-of-factly, anyone would be hard-pressed to say I didn't know it as fact. It was a guess though—supposition.

Grimoires were handed down from parent to child, when the child was inducted into a coven. They were like family cookbooks, but comprised of spells and potions and charms that had been created by the generations past. Rather than recipes for grandma's chocolate chip cookies, you'd find how to give your neighbor hemorrhoids. It was tradition each witch or warlock received their grimoire when they were inducted into their coven, as the mark of the start of their formal magical training. So it was a pretty safe bet the one Tiffani-Amber had in her hand in the video was the one she just received when she became a full-fledged witch.

She turned around slowly, and she looked at me. It was more than a look; it was a question. Did I know? Was I a supe? Another witch? How much could she safely say?

I knew that look. I had given that look dozens of times, unsure of who I was talking to or what. I gave her a slight, knowing nod, and it clicked in her eyes. Tiffani-Amber made her way back to the chair and sat down. "I can explain," she said quietly.

"Please do." I really had only that one card to play, other than the quick change video. Neither were enough to prove she was controlling a zombie and sending it to attack her teachers. I needed her to lead herself there, and the best way to do that was let her talk.

"Just please, don't tell my parents." Her eyes were big and round and reminded me comically of Puss in Boots from *Shrek* when he was trying to look sweet and innocent. "They will kill me if they find out."

I would think her parents would be the least of her worries. The Consortium and her coven would have some pretty severe punishments. She'd be lucky if she wasn't stripped of her powers and thrown into a detention center. "Why don't you start from the beginning," I coaxed, "and then we'll see what we can do."

She sighed and started. "I know I shouldn't be bringing my grimoire out…" A witch's or warlock's grimoire was precious to them and although they could not be taken by force, they still weren't something they carried around in public very often. "…but I needed it.

"I…I…I've been having a hard time in some of my classes. I've got school and cheerleading and now training, and I have like almost no social life because of all these things. It's awful. There just aren't enough hours in the day.

"My grades are not as good as they used to be. I'm used to being a straight A student."

Lies.

"With everything else I have to do, my grades have suffered. I've even got some Cs."

And some D's, I wanted to add.

"I've tried coming in early to get help, but cheerleading practices get in the way. But if I don't bring my grades up, my GPA is going to be too low. And then I won't be allowed to cheer. And if I can't cheer, I'll be replaced as captain.

"And then there's my new training… it's hard. My grandmother just doesn't understand what it's like being a teenager. By the time she was my age, she was already married and had my dad. She thinks schools a waste of time. And cheerleading she thinks is utter nonsense."

Tiffani-Amber took a great, big shuddering breath before she continued, "I've got homework and studying for tests and cheer practice and creating new routines for regionals and then training with grandma and coven meetings. I already have to retake my level one because I didn't practice enough or something. I didn't know what to do."

She stopped and looked at me expectantly, like I was supposed to have a response to her venting—or a solution. This wasn't making sense. I knew there were different levels of magic. Aunt Cassandra was a level seven—the highest level—and she was very proud of that fact. There was no way a witch who failed her level one would be able to raise a zombie. Level one witches were kindergartners reading 'See spot run.' Level seven witches were quantum physicists in comparison. Necromancy was up there with quantum physics.

"Go on," I encouraged her hoping something would start to make sense.

"I guess I don't know what else to tell you," she said as she looked down at her hands. "I mean, that's why I had to bring my grimoire. A speed up spell is complicated. I tried to memorize it, but it was no use. With all the stress, I just couldn't remember it on my own."

"A speed up spell?"

"Yeah," she continued still engrossed in her professionally manicured nails, "to make time for studying and homework. I'd ask to use the restroom during class, find an empty bathroom, then perform the spell. I sped up time about twenty times normal time. I could spend twenty minutes going over my notes for a test or doing homework or even studying spells and only a minute would go by. I could be back to class in no time.

"It's an exhausting spell. I could only do it once or twice a day, but it helped. I finally felt like I was catching up. You know? Like maybe this year wouldn't be a disaster. I even was getting closer to not needing my grimoire. But then…"

Tiffani-Amber glanced up at me, and I saw something I didn't expect to see—a tear trickled down her cheek. She quickly swiped it away with the back of her hand and looked embarrassedly back down.

I admit, I started to feel bad for her. Sure, she was arrogant and snotty and thought she was above the rules, but she was also human. And I was definitely beginning to think

120

there was no way she had raised a zombie… unless this was all a ruse.

"But then what?" I prodded.

"Mr. Durban… Mr. Durban took it," she sobbed. "He took my grimoire. He said there were no 'non-textbooks' allowed in school, and I could have it back at the winter break, but I'd never heard anything about that before." The words flooded out of her in a torrent. "I tried to argue with him, but it was absolutely no use. He insisted that was the rule. And what was I going to do? Go to the principal and tell him Durban took my grimoire when we didn't even have a principal? I told him I'd take it to my car and never bring it again, but he said he was tired of me 'flaunting the rules.' What does that even mean? I follow the rules just like everyone!

"I tried to explain that to him, that I didn't flaunt rules. And told him I would never bring my book back to school again. He said that that was fine, but I'd have more than enough time at home to read it—while I was suspended. Then he started to walk away. All I could think was if I got suspended, I'd for sure be kicked off the squad."

She took a deep breath and then looked up at me pleadingly.

"Please don't tell my parents. Please! They're going to kill me if they find out I took it to school! And my coven, well I'm sure I'll be excommunicated for letting a non get ahold of my grimoire. But what was I supposed to do? I had to give it to him. If he had tried to take it from me, well then he'd have been cursed, and then I'd be dealing with the Consortium…"

And that's when it the pieces came together for her. Her eyes widened, and I saw the knowledge settle in as to who I was.

"You're not with the school district; you're with the

Consortium."

It wasn't a question. It was a statement. And I nodded my head slightly in acknowledgement. That set her lower lip to trembling.

I knew what she was thinking. She was thinking I was there because she let a magical artifact get into the hands of a non-magic person. That was a pretty serious offense. She could be excommunicated from her coven because of it, plus suffer penalties the Consortium imposed. However, I think given the extenuating circumstances, she'd likely just be temporarily suspended. But I'm sure she didn't know that was an option, by the look on her face and the fear in her eyes.

One thing was certain, there was no way she was in control of the zombie. Maybe I needed to talk to Tom again. He was at both attack scenes, including being in that locked stairwell for some reason. He already had incidences of physical violence. To be honest, he did have that 'studies black magic in his parents' basement vibe' too. Was he sick of being pushed around by the teachers who were failing him?

Maybe that sallow complexion wasn't just malnutrition. Maybe it was an after effect of learning black magic? It would also explain the dark circles under his eyes. Most dark witches and warlocks had trouble sleeping, because their dreams were plagued with their victims. The lack of sleep took an already mentally unstable person and eventually turned them psychotic. I'd seen the physical effects of it before. I virtually smacked myself in the head for not seeing it sooner in Tom.

And here I felt sorry for the kid and actually started to like him. I was such a sucker.

"Listen," I started just as the end of day bell rang and Kieron entered the office, closing the door behind him.

"Oh, hello," he said smiling brightly at Tiffani-Amber.

Even with her half-turned toward him, I could see her

blush. Kieron had that effect on girls when he turned on those pearly whites.

"I can come back, maybe Monday, since the bell—" Tiffani-Amber started.

"No, no stay, beautiful," Kieron said with a wink. "I have something that involves you.

"Jen, have you got to the meat of the matter?" he asked looking at me as he took the seat next to Tiffani-Amber and opened his laptop.

"She knows we're with the Consortium," I confirmed. Again, a slight fib. Technically, Kieron didn't work for the Consortium. He was just 'an approved non.' But Tiffani-Amber didn't need to know that.

"Good. So look what I just found."

Kieron turned his laptop so both Tiffani-Amber and I could see it. It was the newsletter Cassandra had sent me, opened to the first page. There was the picture of the two witches and a wizard being ex-communicated. I was confused, but Kieron was quick to explain.

"I was going back through the newsletter, to see if there was maybe anyone else who could possibly be involved. I was thinking that kid, Thomas."

"That's what I was just thinking about too," I agreed. "He seems like he might be the type—"

"But," Kieron interrupted, "I didn't see him in the photo of all the new coven members. So I just started looking at the whole newsletter and came back to this article." He poked his finger at the laptop screen.

"And there is someone else in this school who could be involved, but it isn't Thomas." He zoomed in on the photo. The faces became slightly more recognizable.

"Wait. Is that?"

"Yup," he confirmed, "Douche Bag Durban. I read the article, just be sure. Sure enough—Carl Durban." Kieron moved the image down to the text where they listed the three people in the photo: Sherry Hallow, Diane Nix and there in black and white—Carl Durban.

"Wait," Tiffani-Amber said as she leaned toward the laptop, her brows knitted together in disbelief, "Mr. Durban is a warlock?"

"Not only is he a warlock," Kieron said, "but, I think he's also trying to climb this high school's organizational ladder, by literally stepping on the competition. According to my new friend Stan in Security, not only has he applied for the principal's job, as did Ms. Pruett, but also, surprise-surprise, Mr. Briggs was up for the job too. Want to talk about motivation to sic a zombie on people."

There it was. The last puzzle piece. And who was the douche bag now? Me! For thinking Tom could possibly be involved! God, I was a jerk for judging the poor kid like that. I heaved a heavy mental sigh.

"Zombie? What zombie?" Tiffani-Amber asked looking between both Kieron and myself.

Chapter 13

It took a bit to get Tiffani-Amber up to speed. And once she knew we weren't after her, she reverted back to her snarky self.

"So," she said standing once again, "if we're all done here, I need to get home. I don't have time for this nonsense. The dance is tonight, and my look is going to take hours to put together. Plus, all the girls are coming over for pictures. It's going to be epic."

"Wait one minute, Miss Blair," I said seriously. "Unless you want me to report your misplaced grimoire to your coven, which I'm sure will then report that to your parents, we're going to need your help."

She turned around, put a hand on her hip, and wouldn't you know it, she started tapping her foot impatiently at me. Ugh. I missed the scared Tiffani-Amber just a few minutes earlier. This one was a pain in the ass.

"What can I do? You're the Consortium? You don't need me."

"Actually, we do."

The plan was for Tiffani-Amber to head home, and we would meet her there in a few minutes. She was at first reluctant to agree, until she realized Kieron would be coming along. Then, all of a sudden, she was happy to have us over. I, needless to say, was not happy about her happiness. If she didn't stop batting her fake eyelashes at Kieron, I was going to rip them from her eyelids.

Me? Jealous? Nah.

Durban had already left for the day, but that didn't matter. We needed more evidence before we could accuse him of something like this. We had the motive. We needed the weapon. And to get the weapon, AKA the piece of rotting flesh walking around and attacking people, getting to Tiffani-Amber's grimoire would be a good start.

I dropped Kieron off at his house, so he could change, and I headed to mine. A quick change into jeans and a t-shirt, and then I headed to the basement.

My house looked like about seventy percent of the homes in our neighbor—mid-century bungalow with white siding. It was not large, just two bedrooms and two bathrooms upstairs, but I had never thought of our house as small. I had always thought it was the perfect size. I mean, how much more space did just my mom and I need?

Like most of the homes in the area, we also had a basement. It was just an entirely open space, other than a half-bath someone had put in in the far corner next to the washer and dryer likely in the mid-70s, judging by the avocado-colored sink and toilet. Shelves lined two of the walls, with totes of items we rarely used. Other than that, the space was only broken up by the support columns holding up the upstairs floor.

Cinder block walls and cement floor meant it was one of my favorite places to play in the summer when I was younger, before we had air conditioning. I remember roller skating for hours around and around the space, the iPod and Bluetooth speakers I had gotten for my birthday blaring some inane pop song of the time, on constant repeat.

A small, dusty piece of orange crepe paper still hung from one of the ceiling rafters and flooded my senses with memories of my seventh grade birthday. My mom had a huge birthday party for me and let me invite everyone in my grade. With a birthday of October 30th, she thought it would be fun to do a costume party. Kieron and I had been friends for about a month following the 'floor hockey incident,' and I admit my crush was pretty hard on him at that time, so I was extra-excited for my birthday.

The basement was completely decked out. Black, orange, green, and purple streamers and balloons covered the ceiling. Fake cobwebs were artfully placed in the ceiling corners. Big, fake spiders with glowing eyes nestled into them peered creepily down on the guests. The shelves of totes were hidden by a long sheet of spooky cemetery scenery my mom had found at a party store. And the fog machine she had rented kept an eerie layer of fog on the floor, so no one even knew this was just an old basement. Everybody came, and everybody was having fun.

It was the best birthday ever.

It was also the birthday Kieron made me cry.

We had been standing together by the snack table. Everyone else was dancing and talking and eating and having fun. I looked cute in my evil Alice in Wonderland costume. He looked amazing as Han Solo. I had made the comment that if only I had been born 12 minutes later, I would've been born on Halloween. And he replied, "Are you sure the doctor's watch wasn't off? I mean your face is creepy enough to have been born on Halloween." He then playfully slugged me in the shoulder.

For some reason, that comment got to me. OK, I was a hormonal 13-year old, which may have had something to do with it. Either way, it sent me quickly heading upstairs, before he could see me cry. My mom had been nearby, refilling the chips and dip and had heard the whole thing. She followed me upstairs, only to find me standing in front of the open fridge, peering into it as if it had all the answers to the universe.

"What are you doing, honey?" she asked softly.

"Looking for something to drink," I replied through a sniff, not turning around.

"Jenna," she said turning my shoulder so I now faced her. I could feel the coolness from the open refrigerator on my back. The look of understanding and concern on her face broke me. The tears that I'd been keeping on the brink of my eyelashes finally spilled over and ran down my cheeks.

Great. Now my eyes would be all red and swollen and my make up was going to be ruined.

"He was so mean, Mom. I thought...I thought we were friends."

She pulled me into a hug, and I relaxed into her warmth. My mom could be a scary, bad ass when she needed to be, but when I needed her to be the soft spot I could turn to, she was always there. I felt safe and loved and home when she hugged me. "I think he was just joking, sweetheart," she said as she soothingly rubbed my back. "I think he likes you very much."

"Then...then..." I sniffled probably getting snot on her shirt, "why would he say I was creepy looking?"

She chuckled, and I felt it reverberate against my cheek. "Oh, honey, sometimes boys his age say stupid things. Heck, sometimes boys much older than Kieron say stupid things. Think of it like him verbally pulling your ponytails. Trust me. He likes you."

I pulled away from her and searched her face. I needed to know the truth. It would be the end of my world if he didn't like me. I would just absolutely die.

Yes, I was a bit of a drama queen at 13. Sue me.

"Do you really think so?"

She smiled down at me, "I know so."

As I stood there at the foot of the basement stairs, now five years later, the nostalgia thick around me, I felt a trickle of a tear run down my cheek. I swiped it away angrily. I didn't have time to reminisce, and I definitely didn't have time to cry. I could miss my mom later. Right now, I had a zombie and a warlock to catch.

What those kids five years ago didn't know was behind the cemetery backdrop and then behind the shelves laden with neatly labeled totes, along the far wall, was a storage area. I walked over to the totes now and moved a green one labeled 'XMAS ORNAMENTS' off the second shelf. Behind it appeared to simply be the cinder block wall of the foundation. I placed my hand flat on the surface of the block directly in the center of the space I had created. It grew warm beneath my touch and then, with a dull, raspy, scraping noise, the wall began to pivot open to reveal the storage area behind it.

The wall stopped once a four-foot opening had been made in the now triangular space. Lights zinged on after a few false starts and illuminated the secret space. Along the real far wall—the wall I assumed was the true foundation wall—were four rows of narrow shelves. Each shelf held a myriad of jars and contraptions and pouches and more. Each had a small placard on the face of the shelf, labeled in my mom's neat handwriting. There was an open spot labeled "Zombie Bite Cure" where the last pouch of ingredients I had in my jacket pocket upstairs would go when the undead biter was finally put to rest. I would need to put in a requisition for another pouch. Or maybe two more. Or three. I had never had to use that potion before, but now that I had, it definitely wasn't something I wanted to run short on next time a zombie turned up.

On the opposite wall that was now jutting out at an angle, was a series of pegs and hooks, where a variety of knives, swords, guns, machetes, stakes, and even a cross-bow hung. The arsenal wall had a few empty spots, where my favorite knives would go, should I ever find something I liked to carry better. Finally, at the far, short end of the triangular storage area, was a short hanging bar with clothing hung across it. Most of it was leather and black. It had all been custom-made for Mom, and it made me think of all the times she turned down ice cream after dinner, saying she wouldn't be able to fit into her 'work clothes.'

I walked into the storage area and grabbed a piece of gold jewelry off the shelf, a small locket and then walked further in and grabbed an outfit from the clothing rack. Before I headed out, I chose a dharb from the arsenal wall, with its back scabbard, and a ninjato with the more flexible back sheath. I exited the area and set my goodies on the banquet table next to the washer and dryer. Normally, I used this table to fold my clothes before bringing them upstairs. It had been used for lots of other things in the past—a temporary location to set my weapons was one of the less innocuous. I crossed back to the open wall, placed my hand on the block and waited for it to close completely, before placing the Christmas ornament tote back in its place.

Twenty minutes later Kieron and I pulled up to the address Tiffani-Amber had given us. She lived in Grande Oaks—the ritziest neighborhood in Elmview. You knew it was going to be fancy when they needlessly add an 'e' to the end of 'grand.' It was a neighborhood of what my mom would've called McMansions. I wasn't sure what that meant really. Did it have to do something with McDonalds? But when she used it, it seemed to mean a big, pretentious house that wasn't a full-on mansions, but definitely houses that were bigger than anyone really needed to have.

These houses were status symbols more than homes. Some looked like they could've been a manor house plucked out of the French countryside. Others had the more classic Frank Lloyd Wright-esque look with square columns and prairie-style window dividers that were more common here in the burbs of Chicago. Some had hand-cut stone fronts, while others were accented in brick. No two were alike, other than in size, which was huge. But it was Tiffani-Amber's house that stood out amongst their ostentatious neighbors.

It was white-white. Now, my house was also white, but when you looked at it, you didn't need sunglasses. Tiffani-Amber's house was pure white, like newly fallen snow that almost gleamed in its pristineness. The crisp whiteness was accented with deep, black, glossy shutters. This antebellum behemoth looked like it was a home that should be in the deep South, on some expansive plantation, but somehow it was plopped down in a well-off, Midwest neighborhood. The house took up at least two lots, compared to its neighbors and was comprised of what almost looked like three buildings connected together.

The center was a large, impressive, two-story affair with expansive porches on both floors and topped with a low-slung, hip roof. A two-story portico jutted out from the center, supported by six, massive, square columns that echoed the columns on the rest of the porches. Black, wrought-iron railing scrolled along the front of both porches, accenting the house with an elegant flair. From the center portico, arced two sweeping, curved stair cases, on either side, that met the cobblestone, circular drive in front of the house.

To the left and set back a bit from the main structure,

was an attached smaller structure that almost looked as if the big Greek revival home had birthed a modest colonial baby. I imagined that to be the 'servants' quarters,' and I was sure I was not wrong. It looked tiny, dwarfed by the main building, but I was also sure it alone was probably twice the size of my own house.

To the right of the main structure was a two-story, cylindrical addition. It too featured the same porches, columns and railing, continuing along its façade from the center building, which made it feel like it truly belonged to the main structure. However, instead of the low hip roof, this part of the home was topped with a shallow, domed roof that simply added to the oddity of it being here in a Chicago suburb.

This was no McMansion. This was a full-on, real-life, bold statement-of-wealth mansion.

Kieron and I walked up the staircase, and I imagined socialite parties where valets whisked away cars worth more than my house and red carpets lined these marble stairs. Before I could even touch one of the gleaming silver door knockers, fashioned in the shape of a gaping gargoyle head, that adorned the massive, inky black double doors, Tiffani-Amber flung both open wide.

"Hurry. Come in," she said quietly and immediately headed to another sweeping staircase, set back and to the left of the foyer, leading to the second story of the home.

Although I knew time was of the essence, I couldn't help myself. I stood there in the ginormous entry and stared in awe. It was more white. White marble floors. White giant columns. White statues and white art knick knacks placed into white niches. A huge chandelier hung in the center of the entry. Thousands of facetted crystals dripped toward the floor in a cascade of elegance and opulence. Each of the crystals reflected the light around the room in delicate white beams.

The only color I could see came from the black, grand piano I spied in the room to my left, tucked into the corner of what I guessed was some sort of modern-day ballroom. This room also featured (surprise, surprise) a huge, white, marble fireplace you could roast a whole cow in. To the right of the foyer, the color came in with the rich mahogany furniture in the dining room that could easily seat 40. But the largest shock of color came with the riot of flowers that looked like someone had robbed an entire florist, stuffed into a huge, white vase, on a white plinth in the middle of the foyer.

I had never seen anything so… palatial.

I looked at Kieron and saw he had the same slack-jawed look of awe on his face I was sure I had.

"Oh, hello," a tall, thin woman said as she came into the foyer, from some unbeknownst part of the mansion. She had long, sleek, dark hair that reached her waist and a complexion that said she never went out into the sun without some serious sunblock. "Who do we have here?"

If the home was impressive and daunting, this woman was even more so. Where Cassandra was unnerving at times, this woman was Cassandra on steroids. She radiated intimidation, from the sharp cut of her crisp, white (shocker!) pants suit, to her sleek, black, stiletto heels that I was sure would feature red soles, should I have the opportunity to look at them. This woman was used to being in control without much effort. That was certain.

"Hi," I said reactively, knowing it sounded lame, but unable to form an actual sentence quite yet, but needing desperately to fill the void of silence that hung thickly in the air around us.

Tiffani-Amber stopped, turned and bolted down the stairs to us. "Mother," she said hurriedly before I or Kieron had time to regain the full power of speech, "these are a couple of people from school. We have to do a history project. They just came by so we could all go over our notes, before we do the presentation next week.

"Come on, guys," she said and grabbed our arms, dragging us toward the stairs.

"It was nice meeting you, Mrs. Blair," Kieron called quickly over his shoulder. "You have a really lovely home."

That brought a smile to the stern woman's face. Leave it to Kieron to charm even a witch's mom.

Tiffani-Amber's room was not what I was expecting. Sure, it was as neat and orderly and huge as the other spaces of the house I'd seen but it was not white. In fact, there wasn't a bit of white anywhere. There was a myriad of colors everywhere but done in a way it all seemed to flow. The floor was covered from wall-to-wall with a light gray, very squishy carpet that felt like it would be quite enjoyable to sit on or maybe lay on. (As if I'd ever find the occasion where that would happen.) Colorful area rugs were artfully placed around the space, indicating different areas of the bedroom. Even the ceiling was painted—featuring a sky that went from sunrise from one side of the room to the inky black sky of night with a smattering of stars glittering against it, over the portion of the room that featured her bed.

A cheerleader's outfit was on a dressmaker's dummy. It was torn and tattered and stained and caked in dirt in places. It was positioned next to a large dressing table with more make up arranged in neat rows, than even the most popular YouTube make up guru. A rolling, ornately carved wooden cart, accented with gold leaf, was placed next to the chair with an array of costume make up, an assortment of

134

scars and burns and wounds prosthetics, glue, and fake blood.

Guess cheerleader zombie was going to come out to the dance tonight.

"OK, my girls are going to be here soon, so let's get this over with," Tiffani-Amber said to me, her arms across her chest.

I pulled the piece of jewelry I had retrieved from storage from my pocket. It was a golden locket. On the cover was etched a compass rose, with tiny purple gems at the north, south, east, and west marks. A white, larger gem was embedded in the center. I unfastened a small scroll of paper that was fastened to the chain.

"This is pretty simple," I said flicking open the locket with my thumbnail. "I need some blood from you, and then you recite this spell. Then the locket will guide us to the grimoire."

"What do you mean blood? Why blood?" Tiffani-Amber asked, her eyes widening in fear.

"Your family's grimoire was created with ancestral blood magic. The same ancestral blood that flows in your veins today. This spell will allow blood to call to blood," I explained but wondered why I had to. This should be something she knew, as a witch. Was she really that clueless?

"But…but…blood magic is serious magic. I don't know about this." Her eyes now dashed around the room, as if she was looking for someway to escape. The fear was palpable now.

"It's OK," Kieron stepped forward. "Just a pin prick, and then it will be over."

"It's either this, or I go to the Consortium right now, to let them know about the missing grimoire," I added.

She hesitated—for quite awhile actually. In fact, I thought for a few moments she was going to simply let me call the Consortium and turn her in. I would've got the blood from her anyway, because the Consortium would force her, but it would just mean a lot more paperwork on my end. Have I mentioned I hate paperwork?

"OK," she finally replied. She took a deep breath, closed her eyes and held out her finger.

I was glad she closed her eyes. She probably would've freaked if she saw the deadly sharp push knife I released from my necklace. Kieron held her hand to steady it, and I nicked her fingertip quickly, before replacing my blade. She opened her eyes, looked at the small droplet of blood that had already formed on her finger, and turned white as the marble in the rest of the house.

"I don't feel good."

And then she swooned. Yes, honestly, swooned—the back of her hand raised dramatically to her forehead, knees crumpling underneath her swoon. Given the house she lived in, I'll give her that it was at least appropriate.

Thankfully Kieron caught her, and I quickly tipped her fingertip into the locket and let the drop of blood fall into one side of the compartment. I closed it and felt the slight hum of expectancy it held, knowing it had a job to do and waiting for it to be told its next step.

"Hey, beautiful," Kieron said soothingly as he swooped her up and carried her over to an armchair next to the window. "Are you OK?"

She smiled up at him helplessly, and I wondered how much of an act this all was. Me? Cynical? Nah.

"I'll be OK. Thank you. I'm so glad you were there to catch me. My hero."

Her fluttering eyelashes were risking my wrath.

"I need you to do the spell now," I said breaking up the goo-goo eyes both of them were giving each other. What? We really did have a zombie to catch. That's all. I swear.

Maybe.

I handed Tiffani-Amber the scroll and the locket. She read the scroll to herself, then took the locket in her left hand and held it over her heart.

> "Blood to blood to find what is mine,
> Find my grimoire through space and through time.
> North, south, east, west,
> No hiding spot shall thwart this quest.
> Lost or stolen or taken away,
> Blood claims ownership forever and a day.
> Invenient
> Quaerer
> Plumbum
> Fove
> Aeternum
> Invenient
> Quaerer
> Plumbum
> Fove
> Aeternum
> Invenient
> Quaerer
> Plumbum
> Fove
> Aeternum!

"Ow!" Tiffani-Amber jumped out of the chair and dropped the locket to the ground, and I could see it glowing red with heat. The purple and white gems throbbed in time with one another, with an eerie inner light. It was as if the locket now had a heartbeat of its own.

I picked it up by the chain and then wrapped it in a handkerchief. Wouldn't do any good to run into scary Momma Blair with a glowing, beating finding amulet. That would've taken way too much explanation, and not just a little bit of lying, if we were to get back to the school in time before the Zombies for Everyone dance became literally Everyone is a Zombie dance.

"We *are* going to need your help, again," I reiterated to Tiffani-Amber. "Because I'm going to bet the grimoire is in Durban's office."

"But, the dance!" she protested. And I swear to God she stomped her foot like a petulant child.

"Get ready for the dance. Tell 'your girls' you need to go early for some reason. We'll get this over with, than you can dance the night away."

"I guess," she conceded. "Kieron, you'll be there, right?"

More eyelash fluttering and a cheeky smile from Kieron in return, and I wanted to barf. And punch one of them. Or perhaps both of them.

Definitely both of them.

We agreed she'd meet us at the school at 6:30. This was after much negotiating on how much time it actually took to become a sexy, cheerleader zombie. I thought no time, because there was no such thing. She argued four hours. We split the difference at two.

With the dance starting at 7:00, 6:30 should be when all the chaperones were in the cafetorium getting the decorations finished up and the food set up for the dance. Hopefully, that would mean we could search the school, with the help of the locket, without anyone noticing us. Of course, if someone did see us, Kieron and I needed to be dressed up, since it was going to be a costume dance.

Tiffani-Amber assured us that not everyone was going as a zombie. In fact, she neatly mentioned her *ex*-boyfriend—heavy emphasis on the 'ex' as she looked directly at Kieron—was going as a football player.

"Can you believe that? A Green Bay Packer! Ick!" she said in disgust. "If he weren't captain of the football team, he'd probably get beat up by the end of the night."

Of course her ex-boyfriend was captain of the football team. Could she get anymore cliché?

I dropped Kieron off at his house. He was excited about getting to wear his costume twice this year. Yes, he actually still went trick-or-treating every year, usually under the guise of taking his younger cousin out. But I knew (and he knew I knew) that he was really in it for the candy.

When I asked him last year if he was going to give his candy to his cousin, he said, "Heck no! I earned this candy! I walked around for two hours and about died of heat exhaustion."

He had dressed up as Bigfoot last year, because he was bound and determined not to be cold, after the year before, where he went as Tarzan. It was 28 degrees and snowing the Tarzan year. It was 65 and one of the nicest Halloweens we'd had weatherwise, when he was dressed up in layers of fur.

Welcome to Illinois in October.

Kieron had been talking about the ninja costume he bought this year for over two weeks. Something about basically wearing pajamas and weird shoes while trying to be stealthy got him jazzed up. Boys.

I, on the other hand, had not dressed up for Halloween since that last birthday party in seventh grade. Maybe it was because I knew the things that go bump in the night were actually real. Maybe I just matured ahead of my time. Kieron said it was because I was a 'fun hater.' Nah. That couldn't be it. I was a lot of fun! When I wasn't busy tracking down things that could injure, maim or kill people.

My next stop after dropping Kieron off was the Halloween Mega Store. It was a pop-up shop that appeared in September every year, but always in a different place, depending on what retail space was empty at the time. Talk about profiting on the misery of others. I imagined they got smoking short-term lease rates for stores that would otherwise remain empty. This year it was in a locally-owned craft store—Einman's Arts, Crafts & More—that had been around since before I had been born. I remember going in there as a little kid and participating in their Sunday Kid's Craft Day program every few months. It was always a special treat to be able to paint and glue and sew and just generally make something with my hands. Sadly, the store had closed its doors last April. Located right in the center of a popular strip mall, I could only guess the Internet behemoths, like Amazon, took down another small business owner.

It was sad.

I walked into the now Halloween shop to *The Monster Mash* blaring over the sound system and garish decorations hanging from the ceiling. The large, storefront windows had been nearly blacked out with a purple paint and the lighting was dim, giving the whole interior of the store space an eerie purple glow. To the right of the center entrance, were three rows of big ticket Halloween decorations. These were the things I'd see in other people's yards and think *'Oh! That's cool!'* and then I'd Google it and see how much they cost and think *'Never mind!'*

A life-sized, animatronic Frankenstein groaned and raised his arms when I pushed the 'Try Me' button. Three life-sized witches cackled and spun around a cauldron, while chanting *"Double, double toil and trouble; Fire burn and cauldron bubble."* for their demo. I wondered what Tiffani-Amber would think of these three, old crones, complete with long, hooked noses, and each featuring a giant wart on their face. Would she take this sort of thing in stride? Somehow I thought not.

A vampire popped up from a coffin, turning and hissing menacingly at me, when I pushed his button next. A clown with a huge, evil grin, carrying an innocent-looking red balloon whipped out a large, plastic knife from his back and laughed hysterically, when I pushed his button. (I admit. I jumped at that one.) I spent a good five minutes pushing each demo button I came to.

What? They say "Try Me;" I have to try them.

A greasy-haired girl a bit younger than me came over, about halfway through my trial of all the decorations and asked if I needed any help. Clearly, I was annoying her. I have no shame though. I now had a burning need to know exactly what each one of them did, so I smiled at her, said "No, thank you." and then pushed the demo button for the band of mariachi skeletons that immediately began to play *La Cucaracha* off-key.

Several minutes later, having pushed the last button— a full, fall-foliaged tree where ghosts dropped down from the limbs and waved around spookily saying, "Booooo!"—I made my way through the remainder of the aisles looking for what I actually came in for. I found the accessories aisle and walked passed the plastic pirate swords, eye patches and even a stuffed parrot. I continued passed the rainbow afro wigs, packages of red rubber noses, and pairs of big, floppy shoes. I passed more wigs of every hair style and color, fake glasses, fake noses, fake mustaches, and fake beards, and even a small selection—although these were anything but small—of fake cleavages and butts. When I finally found what I was looking for, I was surprised there was quite a few styles to choose from. Clearly, this was a popular costume choice. With no patience for deciding between the nuances of a costume accessory, I simply went with the cheapest and made my way to the cash register.

"Will that be all for you today?" the greasy-haired girl from earlier asked, with the underlying message of *You drove me nuts pushing all those buttons and this is all you're buying?!*

"Yup," I replied cheerily, paid and made my way out of the store.

I shimmied into the black, leather cat suit my mom had had hanging in the storage in the basement. It was a little loose in the top, but other than that, it was a pretty good fit. It was a little surreal putting on a piece of clothing not only that my mom had worn (I did that anytime I needed dress clothes), but that I knew she had actually 'worked' in. I had seen her go out in this outfit many times. If it could talk, I'm sure it would have some amazing stories to tell. I hoped to add to those stories tonight.

I put on a pair of black, knee-high boots, grabbed the dharb and the ninjato, sheathed in their respective sheaths, and headed for the door. As soon as I touched the garage door handle, I remembered—

Crap!

I turned around and went back into the kitchen. On the counter was the small orange plastic bag from the Halloween Mega Store. I took out my purchase, unwrapped it from its cellophane packaging and then put the black eye mask and black, velvet kitty cat ears headband on my head. I peeked around the corner to the mirror in the foyer. With my hair left loose but sleeked and long, I was going more for Julie Newmar rather than Michelle Pfeiffer or Halle Barry. I doubted anyone at the dance would get that I was Catwoman, but at least it was now a costume. No matter how ridiculous I

142

felt.

"For me?"

Kieron's eyes were the size of saucers when he saw the ninjato. He was already decked out in his pajamas... I mean, his ninja costume. The costume itself looked pretty authentic. There was none of the added plastic, Shogun warrior armor pieces I was used to seeing on little kids that came to the house on Halloween night. His outfit was simple, loose-fitting black pants and top. He had knee-high boots on as well, but his were soft leather, and featured the odd big toe section that screamed ninja footwear. His pants bloused a little over the top of them.

Leather pieces ran down the length of the outside of his arms. He showed me the short leather vest-like piece that would have protected his torso. It featured several buckles in the front. However, he decided not to wear it.

"It's really too hot to wear, especially for a dance."

"You realize we're not going there to dance, right?" I was proud of myself for not going with a Bigfoot costume dig as a reply.

"Oh, I know... but, after we've caught this zombie, you're going to dance with me," he said slyly with a saucy wink.

I had nothing against dancing. In fact, I was known to do some amazing moves, when no one was around, in my own home—with the curtains tightly drawn. But I really hadn't had much experience dancing in public. And the thought made me a bit uneasy. Sure, I was a superstar alone, but I was also pretty sure I looked more like someone who was being electrocuted with a cattle prod than someone who really knew how to dance. Most of the school dances I had gone to were comprised of me standing off to the side, talking to Kieron. And for the dances where he actually brought a date, I simply didn't go.

"I don't know," I said.

"Come on," he said as he grabbed me, his left hand capturing my right hand while his right hand snaked around my waist, pulling me tight against his chest. He began to sway to unheard music. "At least one dance," he leaned in and whispered in my ear.

His breath was warm and sent gooseflesh across my whole body. I could feel his heart beating against mine. I was glad he wasn't wearing that stupid, leather chest piece. He was solid and strong, and as we swayed there in his living room, all I could think about was how easy it would be for me to subtly pull back and kiss him again.

It seemed he was thinking the same thing, because he leaned his torso away from mine just enough to look into my eyes. My lips parted out of instinct—an invitation I was hoping he'd accept. He smiled a small, knowing smile. And my heart sped up in response. Slowly, so very slowly he began to lean in. Nothing else mattered in this moment. There was just Kieron and me and our bodies swaying in unison and his lips inching closer.

"OOoo! These are nice! Where'd you get these?" Kieron's mom said, scaring me half to death.

She had walked into the room and picked up the ninjato. She was about to pull the extremely sharp, cut you just by looking at it sword from the sheath, when I quickly grabbed it away from her.

"Sorry, Mrs. Nicholls. They're from a prop shop near the city. A friend of mine works there. He said we could borrow them as long as we kept them sheathed. He said something about the handles not being attached very well. They're supposedly really expensive to replace."

"Oh, I'm so sorry!" she apologized. "Well, these will be great additions to your costumes.

"I'm heading out. Kieron, Dad should be home soon. If he's not here before you guys need to leave, there's a casserole in the oven. Be sure to eat something."

With a hug to both of us, she was out the door as quickly as she had entered the living rom.

"Well, that was awkward," Kieron said.

Understatement of the year.

"Yeah," I chuckled nervously, "a little."

"I mean, she almost pulled that sword out. She would've totally known it wasn't a prop if she had."

Oh, yeah, that's what he was talking about. Swords. Not almost kisses. Nope. Swords were way more awkward.

"Right. So let's get you some practice in with it, so you don't cut your head off drawing it."

Obviously, the mood was over.

Chapter 14

We arrived at Elmview South at 6:15. I had been taught since I was little that if you were early, you were on time. If you were on time, you were late. So force of habit had me most places at least 15 minutes early. This was a good thing, because we were there before security was stationed at the entrance, which meant no metal scanners to go through.

Although I could've played the School District employee card, I didn't know if that would be strong enough to convince a security guard to let two relatively unknown people into a crowded high school dance with two very deadly weapons. I had considered calling Pringle to make sure he cleared it, but then school employees talk, and I'm sure before we even got to the high school every faculty member would be questioning why we *had* to have real weapons. So instead, I had planned on opening a side door and having Kieron sneak them in. But no security at all and walking in the front door was much, much easier.

Even as I got out of the car, I could feel the pull of the locket in the small, zip pocket on the hip of my leather suit. That was a good sign. I had feared for a few minutes, on the drive over, that maybe Douche Bag had taken the grimoire home, and we'd have to convince Tiffani-Amber to ditch the dance altogether to search his house or somewhere else entirely. But the pull I was sensing meant he hadn't. It looked like the night was going to go in our favor.

Or at least that's what I thought until it was 6:45, and there was still no sign of Tiffani-Amber. I tried calling her, but it kept getting pushed right to voicemail.

So rude.

After the third failed call attempt, I sent her a text—

Where are you??
OMW gheez

I swear this girl was going to give me a headache just from all the eye rolling she was causing me. Did she not even have a clue to how important this was? That lives were literally at stake? Or was she simply so shallow and so self-involved that she just didn't care?

I had taken off my mask—left the ears on though; I admit, they were kind of cute and did keep my hair in place nicely—because it was messing with my peripheral vision. I could just see the edge of the eyeholes when I looked straight ahead. So off it went. I'd just have to be maskless Catwoman. Kieron too had foregone the head piece of his costume, stating it was, like the leather chest piece, too hot to wear for a dance. I wasn't going to argue with him on that one. If the opportunity struck again to kiss him, I didn't want him wearing that thing. It only had a slit-like opening for his eyes. No access to lips for kissing.

While we waited in my temporary office, for Tiffani-Amber to oh-so-kindly make her appearance, I took the locket out to see where it pointed. The locket itself was still hot to the touch and the gems still pulsed in their almost heartbeat-like fashion. There was something very alive about it, and I wondered what magic had actually gone into its creation.

Sitting behind the desk, I held it by its chain directly

in front of me. Blood called to blood, and the locket gently swung diagonally to my right and out in front of me. It was pointing toward the center of the side wall—the wall that joined Douche Bag's office to this one, but also beyond that was pretty much the entire school.

As the locket got closer to its target the stronger it would pull. So if the grimoire were really close by, it should be pulling hard enough to be parallel to the ground. The further away the grimoire was, the less the pull would be on the locket. Right now it wasn't pulling very hard at all. I had only used the locket one other time, with my mother, to actually find a child that had been stolen by some fairies, with a changeling left in its place. With the slight angle on the chain, I would definitely say the grimoire was somewhere in the main body of the school, not as close as any of the administration offices. It looked like we were going to be doing a bit of searching tonight. I only hoped it wasn't hidden in the cafetorium.

And that was if Tiffani-Amber ever got here.

I stood up and walked toward the door to see if I could get a stronger read or at least narrow down which side of the school we should be searching.. Kieron's eyes followed me. As I moved, the locket slowly began to move in the opposite direction, staying focused on the center part of the wall.

I tried to envision what was passed the wall, beyond the admin offices. Definitely the cafetorium was that way. The kitchen too at the far end of the cafetorium would be included in a possible search area. Then there was Corridor D and maybe even some of Corridor C in the swath of possibility.

That was a big area. But with the locket, it was a little like the Hot and Cold game we used to play when we were little, which made it a lot easier.

Just before seven, Tiffani-Amber decided to grace us with her presence.

Here

A one-word text was the pronouncement of her arrival.

I told her to go through security and tell them she was coming in early to help set up with the decorations for the dance. But we would meet her at the administration reception door and let her in there, as soon as she went through. Kieron and I exited the office and made it to reception, but just as I was about to open the door into the admin reception area, it flew out of my hands. Mr. Douche Bag Durban entered in a rush, stopping short at the sight of us.

"What are you two doing here?" he asked eyes narrowed. He was wearing a red button down shirt, and what I assumed to be the same black slacks he had on earlier in the day. He had a short red cape fastened around his neck and two devils horns poking up through his gray-streaked hair, although I couldn't see a headband holding them. I wondered for a moment if he had magicked them onto his head. Either way, it seemed he went out of his way about as much as I did for his costume choice.

"We're with the school district, remember?" I prompted him. "The coyote attack on Ms. Pruett."

"Hmm… yeah. I remember you from earlier. I just feel like I've seen you two somewhere else before. I swear you look—"

Crap. We should've kept our masks on.

"Probably at a school board meeting," Kieron offered—echoing what I suggested to Durban earlier. Great minds think alike.

"Maybe," Durban replied skeptically and then headed

back toward his office, pulling his cell phone from his pocket.

With Douche Bag Durban momentarily out of the area, we re-opened the admin office door and let Tiffani-Amber in. She looked around cautiously.

"Did you guys see Durban? I literally bumped into him in the parking lot when I was texting you I was here. But I don't think he recognized me, thank God!"

It was easy to see why he wouldn't recognize her. Tiffani-Amber was wearing the cheerleading outfit I had seen on the dressmaker's dummy. It was more torn and dirty and stained than it was earlier though. Any of her exposed flesh was a ghastly shade of light, grayish-purple. Patches of skin looked like they were peeling off, revealing red, oozing flesh underneath. There were maggots in these open areas, adding to the gore factor. Her hair was tied into two lop-sided, ratty-looking ponytails. The cheerleader ribbons on each were dirty and tattered. Sticks and leaves stuck out from odd angles of her hair, and her hair was dull and lifeless, instead of its normal, healthy sheen.

Her previously pristine nails were chipped and broken and half-painted. I wondered if she had done it herself or had a manicurist actually make them look like she hadn't had a manicure in years. Her face, though, was the best part.

No one would ever normally describe Tiffani-Amber as anything but thin, but tonight her face looked absolutely emaciated. Her cheeks were hollowed out. Her eyes looked huge and sunken deep into her skull. Her cheekbones protruded unnaturally in a skeletal-like fashion. The same light grayish-purple tone served as the base color, but this was contoured with deep purples and blues and blacks. Her forehead showed a bullet wound, complete with blood and brain matter oozing down the side of her temple, down her cheek and dripping on to her chest.

"Whoa! You look awesome!" Kieron said in amazement.

It really was awesome. I had to hand it to her.

"I know," she replied with a little shrug and a smirk.

"Who'd have thought a dead cheerleader could be so hot?"

I couldn't control my eye roll.

"Alright, we have work to do, since we're already a half-hour late," I said breaking up the love fest before it could begin.

Kieron, to Tiffani-Amber's chagrin, headed back to the security room, to keep an eye on the live video feeds, while Tiffani-Amber and I quickly slipped back into my office. It wouldn't do us any good if Douche Bag saw the two of us together tonight. That would lead to questions I didn't think I could answer, especially since he was already suspicious of me.

I pulled out the locket and showed her how it worked. I explained to her what areas I thought were beyond the point of the locket and asked her if I was missing anything. She agreed that those would be all the areas in that general direction. We made a plan to start with the admin offices first and then keep walking in the direction the locket directed us, as soon as Durban left.

It was the longest five minutes of my life, sitting there with Tiffani-Amber. She huffed every ten seconds in irritation, just to ensure I knew exactly how displeased she was. Multiple times she questioned why she needed to be here at all. And multiple times I reminded her because when we did find the grimoire, she needed to be the one to take it, since it technically was still hers. Finally, when I was about to snap and tell her to shut up and stop whining, I heard a muffled man's voice out in the hallway. I heard the soft sound of the door to Durban's office closing, and I heard him continue to talk as he walked passed my door and out of the admin area.

"Can we go now?" Tiffani-Amber asked impatiently already standing by the door.

"Shh!" I warned her.

I gave it another thirty seconds before I peered out into the hallway, to see if he was gone. The low, thudding bass from music in the cafetorium let me know the dance was in full swing. It was amazing that you could hear it here, with the administration main door closed. The coast was clear. I motioned Tiffani-Amber to join me and took the locket from my pocket once again. It immediately pulled forward and to my right, so I walked forward expecting to walk down the hallway then having to turn and then make my way out of the admin area and into the main part of the school. However, as I passed Durban's office door, the locket swung ever-so-gently back.

I stopped.

It didn't make sense.

Normally, I would think this meant the grimoire had to be in Durban's office. But the locket was still at about a 45-degree angle, which meant the grimoire wasn't that close. I closed my eyes and tried to imagine what was in that direction, beyond the office. Not much.

There was the grassy area with that gorgeous tree directly outside my window that should border Durban's too. Then there was the drive from the front parking lot that led around the school. Beyond that was the cornfield—

"Are we standing here for a reason? I really do have better things to do tonight." Tiffani-Amber's irritated voice cut into me.

I opened my eyes and took a breath. I wanted to tell

152

her this really was all her fault. She shouldn't have given Douche Bag her grimoire. If he had been excommunicated from the coven, they would have confiscated his grimoire. That meant it would be really, really rare that he would be able to pull off the intricacy of a necromancy spell without a grimoire to follow.

He wouldn't have been able to physically take Tiffani-Amber's grimoire from her, not without suffering some pretty severe magical consequences. So now two people had been attacked and almost killed, all because she didn't want to jeopardize her standing as head cheerleader. I wanted to tell her how incredibly selfish she was then—and was being right this very moment—when people's lives were at stake.

I kind of wanted to punch her in the throat, if I was being honest with myself.

Instead, I explained my conundrum in as patient and non-condescending voice as I could muster. "Have you been watching the locket? It's acting like we need to go through Durban's office."

"So? He probably has my grimoire in there. Where else would he have put it? I don't know why you're so confused."

My jaw clenched biting back the response that wanted to fly passed my lips. *Patience, Jenna, patience,* I thought to myself, closed my eyes slowly then reopened them.

"I'm confused because if it were that close, the locket would be pulling harder than this. With it at this angle, it's at least a couple hundred feet away. And there's really not a great hiding spot for a grimoire out there."

"Well, the warding's probably messing with it," she said simply.

And I felt like an idiot.

Crap.

She was right. Warding wouldn't prevent this level of

blood magic from working, but it could obscure it slightly. I hated that she was right. I really, really, *really* hated that she was right. But it meant that this may be as easy as finding it in the office right in front of us.

I tried the door handle, but it was locked. Not a surprise and one of the reason why I made the little witch—yes, that's with a 'W'—miss out on part of the dance.

After a few failed attempts—Tiffani-Amber was definitely no Hermione Granger—we finally heard the lock click open. We slipped inside and shut the door behind us. Tiffani-Amber made to flick on the light, but I stopped her. There was a window on the back wall, just like in the office I was using. And although the blinds were drawn, someone on the outside could definitely see if the light was on. Just in case Durban had gone outside, I didn't want to take any chances.

We followed the locket deeper into the office. It was similar to the one I was in, just a bit smaller. There were three filing cabinets on the left wall. The same desk I had was positioned in the back of the office, with the same two uncomfortable wooden chairs facing it. However, instead of the modest, ergonomic, office chair behind the desk I had been using, Douche Bag Durban had a large, plush, leather, executive chair. It was thickly padded and looked like it should come with a cushy ottoman as well. I looked at it a little closer, and saw a little control pad on the arm. Was that a *massage* chair? Somehow I guessed this was a personal purchase, not a school purchase.

At least I hoped so.

Durban's desk was littered with papers and folders. Mingled in with the papers were two Diet Coke cans and a super-size cup from the hamburger shop down the street. A dirty napkin sat next to it, as did an open burger container with only a smudge of ketchup left in it. There were two plastic paperwork bins on either corner. One was labeled

'IN;' the other was labeled 'OUT.' There was nothing in the out box, but a stack of paper and files in the in box. The desk was a mess, to say the least, and it clearly looked like Durban was falling behind in his job.

On the right-side wall was a large wooden armoire. It was highly polished, made of cherry, and had ornate, scrolling embellishments along the edge. It sat in stark contrast to the other institutional, utilitarian furnishings. This too, I guessed, was a personal piece. And, as we walked further into the room, the locket swiveled toward it.

"I think it's in there," Tiffani-Amber half-whispered.

Thanks, Captain Obvious.

I reached for the knob and pulled knowing ahead of time it would be locked. Tiffani-Amber reached forward to try, but before she got within six inches yanked her hand back.

"Ow! Definitely warded. You can't feel that?" she asked.

I reached forward again and touched the knob, then ran my hand along the surface of the door. It felt like a normal old armoire door to me.

"That is so weird," she said narrowing her eyes suspiciously at me. "As a non, you shouldn't want to touch that door at all. The warding should be like a revulsion to you. Like 'Eww! I don't want to touch that!' kind of thing, you know?"

She reached out again, more tentatively this time, but yanked her hand away giving it a good shake in approximately the same spot. I knew warding was like an electric fence to supes, but this was the first time I'd seen one encounter a ward in person. Tiffani-Amber, to my chagrin, was right again though. A non, like myself, should have the urge to do anything but touch a ward.

"Maybe it's the locket," I surmised. Tiffani-Amber

looked doubtful. "But it really doesn't matter. What matters right now is we need to get into this armoire." I tucked the locket back into the little pocket and wondered if I was going to have to call the Consortium, or worse—Aunt Cassie.

She'd already done me a solid with the newsletter. If I had to call her for this, she'd think I was totally incompetent. She'd probably be disappointed in me. Worse, she'd probably think my mom would be disappointed in me.

"I guess I'll have to do it," Tiffani-Amber said disdainfully as she lifted the side of her cheerleading skirt.

What? I looked at her in disbelief. What did she mean she'd do it?

Strapped to the outside of her thigh with a black, lacy garter was a crystal and silver flask, with an amber liquid inside. "Wrong side," she said more to herself than me.

She lifted the other side of her skirt, where a matching garter held a silver case, about the same width and height of a cell phone, but three times as deep. She opened the case and placed two, thin, black candles on the floor, about six inches away from either corner of the armoire. They looked like longer versions of black, birthday candles. Somehow they stood upright despite their small base, without means of assistance. Next she took out a small incense cone and placed it between the two candles. She set a lighter on the floor in front of the candles and the incense. Lastly, she took out a ring and placed it on the middle finger of her left hand. A large, square-cut garnet, about the size of a quarter, was set into the ring, and it glowed with an preternatural, flickering, inner light, as if there was a candle flame trapped inside it.

I watched in fascination. I had been around supernatural stuff my whole life. I'd seen more strange things in the last 17 years than most people will see in movies in a lifetime. But the one thing I didn't get to see very often was a real ritual. Ritual magic was so very rare and so very private.

Magic was divided into several subcategories. Spells were the simplest and consisted of mostly words with magical intent behind them. Sometimes they included movements or items to help direct the magic, but for the most part they were words—sometimes spoken, sometimes unspoken, and sometimes done as a group or coven for the most powerful of spells.

Nons with even a small amount of latent magic could sometimes perform spells, when their focus was strong enough. I remember my mom and I watched a show on Netflix about focusing on something you wanted and it would come true. They used the example of focusing on getting a good parking spot in a crowded parking lot and how the universe would make it happen. We tried it, and it worked! It became a thing we did, especially during the holidays when even the grocery stores were packed. And many, many times, it worked. A rock star parking spot right up front would open up, just as we drove up to it. My mom thought it was simply the law of averages and luck. Cassandra explained it was simple spell magic and that somewhere in our family tree we must have had a witch or a warlock. Whichever it was, it was pretty cool.

Potions and charms were common magic also, although they took a full witch or warlock to produce. They were similar to one another in that they relied heavily on ingredients combined with a magical intention. The biggest difference was potions were mostly liquid while charms were mostly dry ingredients. Potions often had non-liquid ingredients in them, and charms could have wet ingredients added to them, but the majority of their composition determined if it were a potion or a charm.

Then there were magicked objects. These objects were imbued with magic, either through spell or charm or potion, or sometimes a combination of the three. They often needed a catalyst component to activate them, unless they were meant to be used immediately and for the short-term. The locket was an example of a magicked object. It only had power once blood was added and the spell was cast. But even that power was temporary. I could see the locket starting to flag, lowering itself as the power in it waned.

Lastly, there were rituals. Rituals were the most complex works of magic. They were usually created by only the most powerful witches and warlocks and then passed down in their grimoire to their descendants. They also often involved some sort of magicked object the creator imbued with a piece of their magic, to ensure their descendants would always be able to perform the ritual. It was a high price for a witch or warlock to pay, giving up a piece of their magic. I was told it was like giving up a piece of your soul. But if it were a truly useful ritual, that a witch or warlock would forever be remembered by their descendants for generations to come, it was a form of true immortality.

Because of the power of these rituals and the sacrifice the original creator made, they were also a tightly held secret. A magic family was always worried another witch or wizard would copy their ritual and add it to their magical arsenal. A witch or warlock with a large number of rituals in their grimoire had a certain level of social power, as they were usually the most sought after for marriage, even if they themselves weren't the most magically endowed. Cassandra was on the reverse of this situation. As a new witch for her lineage, she had to create her own grimoire, a process she refused to tell me about. Although she was naturally a very adept witch, she had no rituals in her grimoire—at least none that I knew of that she had created. For that reason, it was unlikely she'd have magical suitors knocking down her door. Of course, I didn't know if she even wanted them, so maybe that was neither here nor there.

Tiffani-Amber either didn't know or didn't care that I really shouldn't be watching this ritual. I definitely wasn't going to remind her. I was fascinated.

She knelt down next to the lighter, in front of the candles and cone of incense. She bowed her head and muttered something so low I couldn't make out what she was saying. She lit the candle on the right and said, "With the power of my ancestors who have gone before me."

She bowed her head again and muttered something softly.

She lifted her head then lit the candle on the left and said, "With the power of my family present."

One last bow of the head and another muttered utterance that sounded like perhaps a prayer or a chant followed.

She picked up both candles in either hand then brought them together to light the incense. Instantly, the little cone tip glowed bright red and started to produce a twisting, thin line of smoke. The smell of sage lightly permeated the air.

"With the power of all my descendants in the future."

Tiffani-Amber placed both candles back in their original spots, but instead of setting them upright, she placed them both at an angle, so the lit ends were angling toward the smoldering incense. The thin candles sat there at a gravity-defying angle, and the incense began to shoot tiny, brilliant white sparks into the air.

I watched in fascination as Tiffani-Amber reached forward and picked up the tiny cone between her thumb and her middle finger of her right hand. Her index finger was stretched out straight. It looked like some odd, fancy way to pick up a teacup. Then, with unnatural grace, she sat back, brought her feet in front of her, crossed them, and then stood, all while holding the miniature firework straight out in front of her, centered on the armoire.

"By the power of the past, present and future generations of Blair magic," she said solemnly as she moved a half-step forward. "I overtake these wards."

The sparks intensified savagely and blinded me momentarily. When my vision came back, I could see they now showered out of the tip bouncing off an unseen forcefield, and cascading down the surface in a shimmering curtain.

"By the magic of my ancestor," she said more firmly, squinting into the dancing light display in front of her, "I crush thee!"

And in one swift movement, she raised her left hand, balled it into a fist, and then shoved the incense cone into the armoire door with the garnet on her ring, crushing it into a flash of searing white light.

Panting, Tiffani-Amber fell back and braced herself against the desk. The black candles lay snuffed out flat on the floor. No evidence of the incense was found, and the armoire looked just like it had moments earlier. I stepped toward it and reached for one of the knobs, and it opened with ease. I was surprised at first, expecting it to still be at least locked, but then realized it would be silly to bother locking it, if you had a ward on it. I opened the door just a crack, stopped and then looked at Tiffani-Amber, because there was something I just had to say to her.

"That was really impressive," I sincerely said to her. And I meant it. Ward breaking was usually only accomplished by the most-skilled witch or warlock. It was normally only a level seven skill, without a ritual. "I've never seen anything like it. It was just… wow!"

"Thanks," she replied as she bent down to pick up the candles and then placed them, the lighter and the ring back into the silver case.

160

"Lucky thing you brought that," I nodded at the case.

"Not luck," she said as if I had just said the stupidest thing in the world. "You would think someone who worked for the Consortium would be smart enough to anticipate a warlock using a ward to hide something. It's not rocket science."

She was... oh, I hated to say this... right again. I *should* have anticipated a ward. I didn't even think of it though. This was the type of rookie move my mom would never have made.

Sigh.

"Well, I appreciate you thinking ahead. Can I ask you kind of a personal question?"

She smoothed her cheerleading skirt over the case, now firmly reattached to her garter and narrowed her eyes at me. "You can ask. I don't guarantee I'll answer."

This was going to be a little insulting, and she probably wouldn't answer it, but I was dying to know.

"You had trouble with the unlock spell on the door, and, from my knowledge, that's a pretty low-level spell. But that ward buster you just did, well, that's some high-level magic, if I'm not mistaken. And you did it perfectly."

I hoped the compliment at the end would take the sting from the insult at the beginning. Thankfully, for my curiosity's sake, it seemed to have worked.

"The ward breaking ritual was one of the first pieces of magic I learned," she began as she sat on the edge of Durban's desk still looking more than a little tired. "My great-great grandmother came to teach it to me and gave me the ring. I'm the first witch in the Blair line, since she was born. They've all been warlocks. My dad was pissed he wasn't given the ring and ritual.

"But, whatever. Anyway, she did what she needed to do to make sure I learned it."

"That must've been some pretty intense lessons."

"Yeah, after she went over the ritual with me a couple of times, she gave me the case and then warded me in my room."

"Really?"

"Yeah. It took me two-and-a-half days to get out."

"You're kidding?! She locked you in your room for two-and-a-half days?"

"And that was after she had infested my room with spiders. Then there was the three feet of water she flooded my room with. But the creepy clowns in each corner were the worst. I definitely had motivation to get the ritual right when they showed up."

I was speechless. What do you say to something like that? Her own grandmother not only locked her in a room, but basically psychologically tortured her. That was all sorts of messed up.

"Don't give me that look," she snapped. "You wouldn't understand. You're a *non*." She said 'non' like it was a racial slur. I knew supes thought they were superior to non-supernatural people, and I had to admit they definitely had some biological advantages. But I had never had any of them verbally spat on me like that. "Let's just get my grimoire, so I can get to the dance. You've wasted enough of my time tonight."

She hopped off the desk, pushed passed me and flung open the armoire doors. Inside was a hanging bar lined with clothing. It looked like Douche Bag kept half of his work clothes here. Three suits hung still fresh in dry cleaner bags, followed by two non-bagged suit jackets and four pairs of slacks. There were a half-dozen button down shirts, a pair of jeans, four t-shirts, and a really ugly, purple velour track suit with a neon orange stripe running down the length of the jacket arm and pant leg. On the floor of the armoire were two pairs of well-worn dress shoes, one black and one brown, and a pair of running shoes that looked like they'd never been worn. The one thing that wasn't in the armoire was the grimoire.

"Where is it?" Tiffani-Amber panicked, shoving aside the clothes and rummaging in the shoes. "It's not here!"

"Let me look."

She backed off a half-a-step, so I could look in the armoire. I carefully looked through each of the pieces of hanging clothing, patting each one down. I was thankful there were no underwear or socks stored in here. Eew!! Nothing was hidden in the clothing, so I moved on to the shoes. I bent over, checking each one carefully. Nothing—except I now knew Douche Bag Durban needed stronger Odor Eaters.

"Maybe it's in your office," Tiffani-Amber sneered her hand planted on one hip. "Maybe you've been wasting my entire evening this whole time, and it was right under your nose all day."

I wanted to correct her on: 1—how dumb that sounded and 2—how if she had showed up on time, we might've been done before the dance even started. But instead I stood directly in front of the armoire, took out the locket again and let it dangle in the center of the space I had made by scooching all of the clothes to one side. I just hoped it had enough juice to give us a clue. I didn't think I was going to be able to convince Tiffani-Amber to donate another drop of blood to recharge it.

Sadly, it hung straight down. Not even a wiggle one direction or another. I closed my eyes, clenched my teeth and dropped my hand to my side. "It's out of power," I said my eyes still closed in frustration and defeat.

"Then why is it pointing?" Tiffani-Amber replied.

I opened my eyes and looked down at the locket. Sure enough, now that it was outside the armoire it was pointing, and quite robustly, right at the floor of the armoire now that the warding was gone. "Move the shoes, one by one."

With each shoe Tiffani Amber pulled out of the armoire, , the locket stayed still. Could it be that simple? "There's got to be a hidden panel." I said as I knelt down and started feeling along the edge of the piece of wood. Sure enough, I found a small hole in the far left corner of the floorboard. It was slightly larger than my finger. I stuck my finger inside and pulled up and removed the piece of wood.

"My grimoire!" Tiffani-Amber cried literally shoving me to the side to grab it. She hugged it tightly to her chest, like it was a lost child.

I put the piece of wood back in place and the shoes. I was just about to tell her to take the grimoire home, and that I'd need a statement as evidence, when I heard a voice coming down the hallway.

I knew that voice.

It was Durban.

"Quick! In here!" I said shoving Tiffani-Amber into the armoire and closing the doors on her. I looked around frantically, but there was only one place for me to hide. I dove around the desk and nestled into the center space between the drawers. I quickly pulled the giant executive massage chair to the desk's edge to seal me in.

I heard the key rattle in the lock and hoped Douche Bag wasn't paying enough attention to realize it was already unlocked. He opened the door and I could hear the music from the dance deep in the background. It quieted again as he closed the door. Durban was talking to someone as he entered, but it seemed to be a very one-side conversation.

"Stop. Good. Open the door," he said as he crossed the office.

People always think you should hold your breath when you're in a situation where you're hiding. However, that's really not the best idea. Sure, at first, no one can hear you breathing, but unless the person you're hiding from moves on quite quickly, you're going to have to take a breath, and it's even harder to make that long intake of breath quieter than your normal breathing would've been in the first place. For this reason, I changed my breathing pattern to soft, quiet, shallow breaths as he came around to the back of the desk.

"Go to your right to D312. That's the one you're looking for. Now wait for my instruction until I tell you to enter."

He pushed the chair back, and, for a moment ,I was terrified he was going to sit down, roll forward and then the jig would truly be up. Instead, he just stood there. I could see his black pants, and his scuffed, black, patent dress shoes. I could smell that those shoes also were in desperate need of an Odor Eater upgrade.

I heard him set something on the desktop. His phone? And then sounds of him rustling around the papers and bins.

"For cripes' sake, where are my headphones?!? Blasted kids with their music," he grumbled. "Why does it have to be so loud? When I'm principal, dances will not be this loud. Last things those little hooligans need is their brains being rattled around like this. Hmmm…maybe I'll just ban all dance altogether!

"Now, where did I put those stupid headphones. I know I left them right on my desk!"

He grew more irritated and the rustling got more intense as he continued his muttering about stupid kids and loud music and how things would change when he was in charge. He picked up a soda can and threw it across the room in frustration. A paper floated to the ground just at the edge of the space I was hiding in. I could've easily reached out and snatched it. But all I could think was, *Please don't pick it up! Please don't pick it up! Please don't pick it up!*

Luckily, the powers that be must've been listening, because he left it on the floor. Instead, he turned to the drawers of the desk. Each time he opened one, I worried he was going to bend just enough to see me. He searched through one drawer, then slammed it shut. Then did the same with the next. Finally, on the third drawer, he must have found what he was looking for, because he slammed it shut and then headed out of the office.

The last thing I heard him mumble to himself as he left the office and closed the door was, "Now to make sure I'm seen."

I waited a count of ten, to make sure he was gone for good, then crawled out from under the desk. Tiffani-Amber came out of the armoire. If it weren't for the ghastly zombie make-up I was sure she would be pale as a ghost right now.

"Go take the grimoire to your house. Don't stop for anything."

She didn't argue and just left, still clutching the grimoire for her life.

I tried to call Kieron, but he didn't answer. I sent him a quick text and then rushed off to get to room D312. I wasn't sure what was going on, but I was sure it wasn't anything good.

Chapter 15

The dance was in full swing when I rushed out of the administration offices. What had been a dull *buh-buh-bum-buh* sound in the hallways of the office turned into a full-on, blaring, concert-level of music, as soon as I opened the administration reception doors and entered the entry leading into the cafetorium. My head and heart started to thump in time with the deep bass line, and I had to admit, Durban may have been a little bit right that this music was unnecessarily loud, even for my young ears.

The cafetorium was packed. The standard overhead lights were off and in their place were green floor lighting shining from the edges of the space into the center. This minimal lighting was accented with orange and purple strobe lights that swept over and through the crowd in random patterns.

A stage had been erected, in front of the kitchen area and featured a DJ with a Ghostface mask and headphones on over one ear. All of his gear was positioned on the center of the stage. To either side of him were stone-like plinths with large, fake flaming cauldrons. The fabric flames blowing in the unseen fan housed in the cauldron waved back and forth and were lit by orange lighting within the cauldron itself.

A wall of students seemed to be edging the cafetorium. It was a scene dance goers from any generation were familiar with. There always seemed some kids were dancers and some were standers. Some of those currently standing were chatting with their friends. Others were standing alone looking forlornly at the people dancing or fixedly studying their cell phones.

There was also a crowd around the refreshment tables, with a line of chaperones hurriedly working to refill cups and bowls of goodies. I noticed there appeared to be a couple of chaperones whose sole job was to carefully watch the drinks and snacks, to make sure no one got a little mischievous and tried to spike something. In the center of all this, though, was dancing.

People were crushed together but still somehow able to carve out just enough space to show off their dance moves. Most were pretty harmless. Some were kind of dangerous. Some were quite comical, and some were a bit risqué. But a few dancers were actually quite talented.

I watched a zombie bride and groom cut a pretty large swath out of the crowd, near the wall of standers—giving them a show. The groom took his bride by the hand, swung her out away from him, then coiled her back in tightly. He then bent and lifted her, throwing her over his back and back around his torso, like she weighed nothing more than a sack of flour. The bride was back on her feet and then furled out again, her free arm raised up and out dramatically.

Somebody had definitely taken some lessons.

I would've loved to stay to watch them, but instead I rushed into the throng of costumed dancers. I pushed through the standard issue costumes—Frankenstein, a few witches, a vampire here or there, a guy that had a pretty convincing mid-change werewolf costume going on, someone just wearing a neon green morph suit—but for the most part the place was filled with zombies. They weren't kidding with the *Zombies for Everyone* theme.

Most of the costumes were pretty sad renditions of what a zombie actually looks like (although I had to give a special nod to the Minecraft zombie, with his green painted box on his head.) However, some of the zombies were pretty exceptional. Like Tiffani-Amber, some kids had spent quite a lot of time and money on gory prosthetics and make-up to get that "just dead" look. Many of them were even shambling around, as if they were the real thing. Our actual zombie could be in the middle of this crowd right now, and it would be very hard for someone to spot the difference. Well, at least until it started to chomp on someone.

Even the putrid, rotting zombie smell may be masked in this chaos. Now that our walking dead friend was at least a couple of days old, he should be getting pretty ripe. But the cafetorium was no bed of roses right now on the smell scale. It smelled like old pizza, B.O., cheap perfume, and even cheaper cologne. Couple that with a small hint of rot-gut booze that permeated the air every once in a while, as I wove my way through the gyrating crowd, and I don't think you'd be able to smell the real zombie until it was close enough to be too late.

I was almost at the far edge of standers. I could see the D corridor just beyond. I admit, I was getting a little claustrophobic, so it was like the light at the end of a tunnel for me, when a guy in a Batman costume blocked my path.

"I'm Batman," he said in a hoarse shout over the music, his hands placed dramatically on his hips. "Dance with me, Catwoman."

"No thanks," I yelled back as I sidestepped around him, bumping accidentally into a ballerina zombie.

As I turned to apologize quickly to the ballerina, I felt someone grab my hand and yank me to them.

"One dance," Batcreep demanded.

I twisted out of his grip, grabbed his wrist and

wrapped his arm backward and up around his back between his shoulder blades. He yelped at being chicken winged, and it was my turn to pull him close to me, his back pressed up against my chest.

"Have you ever danced with the devil in the pale moonlight?" I whispered menacingly into his ear. "Don't ever grab a female again."

I let him go with a little shove, and he stumbled forward into a Freddie Mercury zombie who shoved him right back. He rubbed his shoulder with a frown and just goggled at me. As I turned to walk away, he called out, "Hey!"

Thinking it was going to be an apology, I turned briefly back to him.

"That's not your line," he said still a bit stunned.

I chuckled and continued on.

The third floor hallway of the D corridor was empty. The music from the dance echoed through it, more bearable but still loud. I made my way quickly to room 312 and opened the door slowly.

It was a classroom—a classroom that looked like a tornado had gone through it. The desks were scattered about, many of them on their side or upside down. Textbooks were randomly on the floor, lots of them with the covers half-torn from their bodies. But the strangest sight was in the back of the classroom.

In the right corner was a small, Japanese geisha dressed in an ornately embroidered, red kimono. Her glossy, jet black hair was pulled up into a large bun that I was sure was neat and tidy when she started the evening but now looked frazzled with hair pulled out of it in stray bits. The red headpiece she wore was off-kilter and only a small cluster of flowers was left at the base of her bun. The geisha's white make up made her dark red lips and black-lined eyes stand out in stark contrast.

She was standing behind a bookcase that had been pushed over on its side. Oddly, the geisha was brandishing a flag pole and smacking someone about the body and head with it. As I stepped forward, the smell hit me.

That wasn't just someone she was beating with a flagpole. That was our zombie.

It was a short man with glasses, dressed in a filthy, orange jumpsuit that clearly had seen better days. His hair was dark and his skin was the gray pallor of death. His arms were outstretched as he swiped at the geisha. Each time he reached for her, the geisha would bat his arm away and then smack him with the pole. One swing connected squarely with the side of the zombie's head. *THWACK!* I saw the burst of rotting flesh and gore spew from the impact.

Gross!

I began to sneak further into the room. If I could get close enough, I could-

And then things turned bad.

The geisha tried to swat another reach of the zombie's away, but the zombie timed it just right and instead grabbed the flagpole. He wrenched the flagpole from the geisha's hands and tossed it away leaving her completely defenseless.

Crap!

I pulled my dharb from its scabbard, but before I could get to the zombie, a figure in black leapt in from the opposite side of the room. I had been so focused on the zombie and the geisha, I hadn't even noticed anyone else in the room. The figure landed lightly on the end of the fallen bookcase. A slash of a gleaming sword slid easily through the zombie's neck, and I watched in fascination as the head spun around once then flung itself off to the side, like a top that had just been released from its string, before landing with a *CLUNK!* on the floor. The glasses the zombie had been wearing skittered across the floor, landing against a fallen desk. The zombie's body crumpled to the ground, as did the geisha's.

I got to the three of them—the zombie, the geisha and the... Kieron?!?—a moment later. Kieron was already kneeling over the geisha and checking her pulse.

"I think she just passed out," he said. He looked pale and his eyes were dilated.

"You did good," I said with a huge smile. "Who knew you really were a badass ninja?"

Kieron was about to say something, but then leapt back over the bookcase, sprinted across the room and bent over the wastebasket next to the teacher's desk. The vomiting was loud and wet, and I was sure Kieron was now regretting eating that roast beef before we left his house.

"Stand up!" a tiny, tinny disembodied voice said. "I command you! Stand up!"

I looked around, wondering where it had come from.

"For cripes' sake, what is going on?! I said, stand up!" the voice said again.

It was coming from the head.

I walked over and cautiously toed the head with my boot. There was already a slick puddle of fluids pooling up around the neck—definitely not something I wanted to get on my boots. I toed the head over and saw an earbud had come out of one of the zombie's ears. Someone was communicating with it by Bluetooth. Not just any someone. I'd know that voice anywhere—Douche Bag Durban.

But how did he know his zombie was on the ground? I looked around the classroom to see if there was a security camera. Nope. Then I saw the glasses laying off to the side.

Affixed to the bridge of the nose was a tiny spy camera. He must be pulling a video feed from it and assumed the zombie was lying on the floor! Well, he got the on the floor part right.

Kieron had regained control of his stomach and came back to me. "Please tell me we don't have to clean this up," he said pointedly not looking at the zombie.

"No, but Durban is bound to show up at any minute, and there's something we need to do before he gets here."

Three minutes later, we had the tossed desks out of the way of the front of the room, and I had placed six, flat pieces of agate in a circle, on the floor. As we heard the door open slowly, Kieron and I ducked behind the fallen bookcase, with the still unconscious geisha. The last thing I wanted to do was spook him. I needed Durban to come all the way through the door.

"What the—" Durban yelled.

I stood expecting to find Durban trapped in a dome of crystalline power. Instead he had somehow sidestepped the border of the trap and now was standing directly in front of it. One hand clutching his cellphone, he looked at me in utter confusion.

"What's the meaning of this?!" he demanded.

I knew three things in that moment.

He was a dangerous warlock that wasn't' above killing someone.

I needed him in that trap.

And I was no match against his magic.

There was only one thing for me to do. I vaulted over the bookcase and ran straight at him. His eyes went wide in disbelief as I neared to about a foot away, leapt into the air, channeled my inner Bruce Lee, and side kicked him with all my might. The momentum of my run, the force of my leg as my foot made square contact with his chest, and the sheer element of surprise sent him stumbling backward with an exhaled *OOF!*

Right into the trap.

Instantly, a frisson of unseen power set my teeth on edge and caused the hair on the back of my neck to stand up. I stumbled backward away from the trap and watched as Durban's face transformed from disbelief into outrage. With a snarl, he tried to shoulder into the invisible barrier—hitting it hard, bouncing away from it and falling on his butt. His phone dropped out of his hand and slid out of the trap, between two of the agate pieces.

"I demand an answer!' he shouted as he returned to his feet.

A look of realization came over his face. "Wait! Aren't you two the ones from the school district? I don't think you know who you're dealing with! I'm principal of this school, and I expect you to release me right this instant!"

Did he really not question why school district employees would capture him in a warlock trap? I had to roll my eyes at not only his naivete but at his already claiming the title of principal. Yeah, sorry bud, you can kiss those plans goodbye.

"I don't think *you* know who *you're* dealing with," I corrected him. "I'm with the Consortium, and you're being taken in," I said with a smirk.

Hey, there are times when it's appropriate to smirk, and this was definitely one of them.

I asked Kieron to help me make another clearing closer to the back of the classroom and began to slide desks off to the side.

"On what charges?" Durban fumed.

I ignored him.

"I said—on what charges?!" Douche Bag bellowed.

I still ignored him. I knew I wasn't wrong on this one now, so there was no need to even waste my breath on him. He could wait until the clean-up crew from the Consortium got here to move him and formally charge him.

Kieron and I moved the last of the desks over, before I took out my phone. And then Durban did the stupidest thing he could do.

He cast a spell.

I wasn't sure what it was, but the bolt of energy that flew from the palm of his hand was aimed at me. I'm sure it wasn't something pleasant. However, instead of finding its intended target, the spell ricocheted around the inside of the trap. I watched Durban duck and jump out of the way, as the bolt of energy zipped this way and then that each time it struck the invisible dome wall. Although he made a valiant effort at dodging the bolt of power, finally the spell found a victim, and Douche Bag Durban went rigid. He stood there for a moment, the utter look of shock of what had just happened frozen on his face, then he fell over backward.

Again—play stupid games; win stupid prizes.

I shrugged and dialed the Consortium, waving Kieron to come stand by me.

"CES," an elderly lady with bright, white, short, curly hair and a face like a prune answered my video call.

"I have a Code 815 with one likely uninjured but unconscious. Jenna Sutton. 1-0-foxtrot-2-tango-1-6-9-whiskey." I turned my video forward to show the cleared area in the classroom. "Clear to receive."

"One moment," prune-face said, and then the HOLD screen came on.

The air in front of me shimmered and rippled as the call disconnected. With a flash of light, four men and two women appeared.

"Aye, lass, ye just can't get enough of me, eh?" Colm said as he came forward and his team separated to take care of the zombie, the geisha and Durban.

"Something like that," I laughed. "Sorry about the mess."

And there definitely was a mess going on. Not only had the pool of yuck around the head of the zombie increased in size, but there was now a festering puddle of decomposing body to attend to. Without magic holding it together, the body had begun to hyper-putrefy. I wondered briefly what stain remover they would use to get that out of stubby, industrial-grade carpet that covered the classroom.

"Looks like ye got yerself a zombie here. Good work!"

"The killing blow wasn't me. That was Kieron," I said pointing to Kieron. "Kieron, this is Colm McAleer with the Consoritum. Colm this is Kieron Nicholls, my…" I didn't know how to describe Kieron. He was more than a friend, but he wasn't a boyfriend. At least not yet. He wasn't my assistant. Not officially. Side kick? Approved non? Nah, those didn't sound right. So I just didn't finish the sentence and hoped neither guy noticed.

"Nice to meet ye, Kieron, her…" Colm said with a wink as he extended his hand. "Really, fair play on the zombie. I haven't seen a zomb for donkey's years."

"Nice to meet you too. And, uh, thank you?" I was glad I wasn't the only one who was confused by what Colm had just said.

"I best be getting to work. Don't want this lot callin' me a doser," Colm said now looking directly at me. "I'm going to need to get with ye in a bit, Jen, if you can stick around. Need a wee bit of information for the boss, before I bring this mess in. I'm assuming the Japenese lady is a non?"

"She's Chinese," Kieron cut in. "Lin Fucanglong is

Chinese. She teaches Mandarin here."

"How do you know that?" I had to ask.

"Stan, you know I mentioned him—the security guy, he was telling me about her. I asked him if there was anyone else who might be in line for the principal's job. He said Ms. Fucanglong."

"It's a good thing he told you about her, so you came up here and rescued her," I smiled at him.

Kieron blushed, honestly blushed. It was the cutest thing I'd seen in a long time and my heart zinged a little. "It wasn't that. It was the orange jumpsuit.

"I remembered that Tom kid told you that the only way to tell the difference between the two janitor brothers was their jumpsuit. And the one that was at Ms. Pruett's accident scene was wearing orange. But he was supposed to be on vacation, right? So I figured I'd check it out. I mean, he shouldn't have been here," Kieron gave a little shrug like it was no big deal.

The kid had good instincts. I had to give him that.

A moan in the front of the classroom caught our attention. Four of Colm's people had Durban up and in handcuffs that appeared to be made from pure, gold light.

"What am I being taken in for?' Durban muttered groggily at them. "You have to tell me the charges. I know my... rights?" He slurred.

The female member in that group sighed and pulled out her phone.

"You're being taken in on charges of unauthorized use of magic by an excommunicated member of a coven, unauthorized necromancy, attempted murder of three nons, and murder."

"That's ridiculous!" Durban shouted now more lucid. "I didn't murder anyone!"

"I think Alejandro Torres here would beg to differ," I

said pointing at the mushy mess that used to be someone's brother, someone's son. "And please add unauthorized use of another witch's grimoire to the list of charges."

The girl typed the new charge into her phone.

"I didn't murder the janitor," Durban sputtered as two of the CES team began to bind his legs for transport. "He was already dead! I found him in the bathroom stall. Dead. Probably from the cancer he had. I'm not a mur—"

That was the last thing he said before they magicked his mouth shut and the team and captive disappeared. I noticed the geisha—Ms. Fucanglong—was also gone with the person who had been attending her. I thought she had been uninjured, but maybe she had hit her head. Either way, I knew she was in good hands now.

Colm also noticed he was the last of his team there. And the place was still a wreck, including the decomposing body and head.

"Guess that's what I get for standin' here chattin' you up, Jen. Now I've been left with the manky bits. But I do need to have a word with ye, once I'm finished up."

"Let's go down to the dance," Kieron offered, "to get away from the smell. You can wait down there."

The smell was getting increasingly worse. The pungent smell of death was cloying and was getting so bad I could almost taste it. The dance with its blaring music didn't sound half-bad in comparison. We could join the wall of standers and maybe watch the zombie bride and groom dancing.

"That's a good idea," I confirmed. "Colm, text me when you're done, and I'll come back up."

"It sounds like there's a fierce party goin' on out there. So maybe I should stick around a wee bit after. I'll find you out there. No worries."

Chapter 16

The music was still loud and the makeshift cafetorium dance floor was still packed. I led Kieron over to the refreshment table. He still looked a little peaked, so maybe some sugar would help. I forced a cup of Sprite into his left hand, but when I tried to give him a zombie-shaped sugar cookie he absolutely refused. OK, maybe that was asking too much.

I ate the cookie as he drank the soda. By the end of the glass, he started to perk up a bit.

"All these years and we've never danced together. Let's dance," he shouted at me over the music. The song was something techno, and I'd only heard it a couple of times on the radio. People were jumping up and down to it. It wasn't really a 'dance to it' kind of song, in my mind.

"I don't really dance to this kind of music. I'm more of a slow dance girl," I hedged. I really didn't want to dance at all. Kieron should know that, since out of all the dances we had gone together—as friends—and as he said, we'd never danced together. But I didn't want to sound like a complete fun hater, so I figured the slow dancing would be a good excuse. I hadn't heard a slow song played yet—

Crap.

Just as the thought ran through my brain, the music changed tempos and even volume. It was *When Will You*

Realize by Hillary Cantante. It was a song about a boy who never really appreciated the girl in front of him. The boy goes from girl to girl, never happy, without realizing the one he really needed was there all along.

I could relate to the song.

"Here's a slow song," Kieron said and held out his hand. I reluctantly took it and let him lead me into the dance area.

The dancers had thinned quite a bit—apparently slow dancing wasn't that popular here at South. But there were still quite a few couples on the dance floor. Most were smashed against one another, like their torsos had been fused together. A lot of them weren't actually dancing at all, but merely swaying slightly from side-to-side. Some had given up the pretense of dancing altogether and were just standing there kissing.

Kieron pulled me close and put his hands on my waist. I put my hands on his shoulders and we began to move awkwardly back and forth. I tried to let him lead. That was difficult. Apparently I have control issues. Not a surprise. I also had no idea where to look.

Do I look at him? Do I look down at the three-inch gap between us to make sure I don't step on his toes? I was now envious of the girls who were pressed close to their partners. Most of them had their heads resting on their partner's shoulder and had their eyes closed. That would end the where to look conundrum. With no idea where to look, I found myself looking everywhere. My eyes darted around the room. I'm sure if someone looked at my face, I'd look like a crazy person.

"Hey," Kieron said grabbing my attention.

Crap.

Was he watching my crazy eyes? I focused on him. *Act sane. Act normal.* Even in this light I could see how blue his eyes were. I really did like his eyes.

"I didn't tell you how pretty you look tonight," he said with a smile. "Sexiest Catwoman ever."

OK, it was awkward again.

"Thanks," I said looking down at our feet.

He moved one hand up to my chin and tilted my head up to look at him again. Oh, those eyes held me captive.

"We make an excellent team, you and I. I think we always have." It was such a simple statement, but it held so much promise.

His hand was still cupping my chin, and we were so close to one another. He was right. We made an excellent team. He was my right hand. My best friend. My confidant. My rock. Screw waiting for him to kiss me. Ever since he kissed me in the car, I had wanted to kiss him again. I closed my eyes and leaned in to kiss Kieron first.

"Hey, ninja! Can I have this dance?"

My eyes opened to find Tiffani-Amber smiling seductively up at Kieron, her hand rested possessively on his arm. Kieron took his hand off my chin and turned toward her. The song had transitioned into another slow song. I couldn't hear the words for the buzzing anger and frustration that filled my brain.

"You don't mind. Do you, Jenna?" she said a wicked gleam in her eye. Had she known I was about to kiss him?

"Where's the grimoire?" I asked.

"Home—safe. Now, Kieron, dance with me, pleeeease." She gave him big, puppy dog eyes to go along with the whiny 'please.'

Kieron turned to me, about to ask permission. "I'm all danced out," I lied and turned and left the dance area to get another cookie before he could even say a word.

These cookies were actually pretty good and really detailed. Each zombie had his arms outstretched. They had green skin, tattered shirts and shorts, and big bulbous eyes. None of them had hair. I guess the cookie maker assumed all zombies would be bald. They were a nice, crisp cookie, with a slightly soft center. I reached for a fourth… or was it a fifth? I had lost count.

"Care to dance, lass?"

I turned to find Colm standing behind me. I wondered if people thought he was dressed as someone from the 1950s with his black jeans, white t-shirt and black leather jacket. I was about to decline, when I saw Tiffani-Amber toss her head back and laugh at something obviously incredibly funny Kieron had just said.

Screw it.

"I would love to."

We made our way onto the dance floor. Colm took one of my hands in his and placed the other on my waist. It was very formal, and I followed suit by placing my unheld hand on his shoulder.

"Are you ready, lass?"

"Umm…sure?" I said hesitatingly.

And then we danced.

I mean really danced.

We spun and twirled and moved across the dancefloor, my feet magically following his. We flew from one side to the other as Colm looked down at me and smiled. It was glorious, moving with such grace and ease. I could feel people watching us, and I didn't care. I had no worries. Colm was in control, and I trusted him. As we spun in a circular at one corner and I felt the centrifugal force of the move pulling on my body, I laughed. As the song came to an end, we stopped, and I could feel myself grinning like an idiot from ear-to-ear.

"That was fun. Thank you," I said sincerely.

"Pleasure was all mine," Colm replied not letting me go. "I need to go over some details with ye, about the…," he looked around cautiously.

"I think you can say 'zombie.'" I laughed. "We're at a dance full of zombies."

"Anyway, would you like to go for a poke?"

"I'm sorry, a *what?*" I said incredulously. There was being straight forward and then there was being just downright lewd, and Colm had firmly hop, skipped and jumped over that line.

"A…" he thought about it a moment, "an ice cream cone. You know, for afters."

Ohhh!

I laughed again. I hadn't laughed this much in I don't know how long. I was just about to say we needed to take Kieron along when I looked across the room and saw Tiffani-Amber stand up on her tippy-toes to kiss him.

Yeah, forget Kieron.

Maybe I needed to give Colm a chance.

"I would love to go for ice cream. But let's never, ever, ever call it that other thing again."

WEREWOLVES EVERYWHERE

A JENNA SUTTON SUPERNATURAL COZY MYSTERY
BOOK 2

COMING
NOVEMBER 2021

Sign up for our newsletter for special
Jenna Sutton fans
discounts, news and more!
https://www.jennasuttonmystery.com